CANDACE ROBINSON
S.G.D. SINGH

A HORDE OF DEAD POETS

IN THE
HAUNTS
OF
GOBLIN MEN

CANDACE ROBINSON

S.G.D. SINGH

PERCY'S HEART PRESS

To those who were ever curious about tasting the goblins' fruit

Dear, you should not stay so late, twilight is
    not good,
for maidens should not loiter in the glen in
    the haunts goblin men.

Christina Rossetti
"Goblin Market"

Contents

One

KITTY

"Thou shalt not fall into the hellfire of temptation, Maidens, if one never forgets to remain vigilant and always, always beware the goblins' trickery," the vicar said, his voice booming through the church. "Their evil fruit, once tasted, is never forgotten."

Kitty only half listened to the sermon while her gaze drifted to the young man in the pew before her. The back of his neck looked smooth like silk, one small freckle at its center, begging to be kissed. He brushed a lock of curly auburn hair behind his ear with fingers as perfect as any master sculptor could fashion. Kitty blushed at her own thoughts, turning to her Bible. She had fancied Duncan for as long as she'd known him, yet his eyes always drifted toward her sister, Esther. As neighboring children they'd played with stray dogs in the village lanes and made mud pies near the glen on rainy afternoons. Those days seemed long ago now that she was eighteen.

A leg bumped into Kitty, startling her, and she met her sister's hard stare. Kitty rolled her eyes and straightened in her seat, pretending to be captivated by the sermon just as her mother and aunt were doing beside her.

The vicar continued his warning against the demonic goblins, a theme he'd warmed to ever since one of the local women withered away after eating the creatures' wicked fruit. *Foolish woman.* Kitty never understood how one could be warned from the time of early childhood about ignoring the goblins' call and yet still decide to eat the fruit anyway. Perhaps the woman hadn't wanted to live any longer or had been too tempted to discover the fruit's taste.

Only two women had ever survived the goblins and lived to tell their tale: Kitty's mother, Laura, and Aunt Lizzie. She glanced at her mother out of the corner of her eye, wondering what she'd looked like as her body lay withering and aged, her starving form nearly bones. If it hadn't been for the bravery of Aunt Lizzie, her mother would've been sacrificed to the Goblin King, her soul trapped in his realm for eternity.

"And that is the conclusion of today's sermon," the vicar said, his gaze meeting Kitty's as though he knew she hadn't paid him her full attention.

"Come on, girls," their mother said, clinging onto her Bible. "Let's have a picnic for lunch, shall we?"

Aunt Lizzie brushed her hands down the front of her dress. "That sounds delightful, Laura." But something in her eyes remained empty, just as they had been ever since her husband died in the war, alongside Kitty and Esther's father. And it was only a year ago that Aunt Lizzie's son had grown ill, his tiny body wracked with fever until he passed away. At some point another streak of gray had been added to her beautiful blonde curls.

Duncan turned around and gave a bashful grin to Esther.

"We have a batch of new apples. They'd be perfect for your pies if you want to come by the market tomorrow?"

Esther smiled politely, but only said, "Sure, I'll send Kitty."

"See you then, Kitty." Duncan's expression never wavered, but the spark of hope vanished from his eyes.

As they left the church, warm sunlight broke through the clouds. A flock of pigeons called to each other as they flew past. The day was perfect for a picnic as the four of them walked home along the winding trail to their meager cottages. Aunt Lizzie's home was on their property, but both cottages were in need of work. Even with the number of pies their bakery sold, there never seemed to be spare coin to spend for repairs. Thankfully Duncan had been willing to lend a hand, when he wasn't working at the market or tending the fields of his parents' home.

The chickens squawked and pecked at their feed in front of the cottage, and Kitty sat beside Esther on the stairs as her sister read a letter she'd received from her friend Winifred, who'd married and moved away to London the prior year.

"Duncan will notice you one day." She bumped her shoulder into Kitty's. "I promise."

"If you fall for him, I won't mind. You deserve happiness." It was half a lie, but Kitty did want to see her sister's dreams come true. If only her own could come true as well...

They ate cucumber sandwiches and sausage rolls, while laughing about the neighbor's pig getting loose and other bits of minor town gossip, until it was time for Aunt Lizzie to go home.

Aunt Lizzie gave the sisters each a hug goodbye, then became serious, as she always did before departing, her words so familiar to Kitty they had become a bore.

"I strengthened the wards on the windows," she said, "so make certain to say your prayers after kissing your iron crosses before you sleep." The goblins were said to fear iron the most.

"We never forget." Esther nodded.

"Of course we will," Kitty added. Women didn't vanish that often, and even though Kitty knew goblins would of course never come to them, she repeated her prayers every night if not for herself, then at least for her aunt and mother's comfort.

That night, Kitty lay in bed, peering up at the ceiling. "Protect us from evil. Protect the women in our village from those who would harm them. Draw us close to your heart, Lord, that we may not fall into the temptation of evil. Save those who have fallen by the hands of goblins before us—may their souls rest in eternal peace forever."

Two

ESTHER

The village rooster was silent that morning. It was the first thing Esther noticed as light seeped through the lace of her curtains. She thought that perhaps a fox had absconded with the poor creature, but as she sat, fully awake, her unease mounted.

The house was still. Unnaturally still, as if air itself had ceased to exist within its walls. It had never been this quiet. Not once had her mother failed to rise before Esther, who found her busy baking in the early hours of each day. Esther thought about yesterday's sermon. The goblins—nothing but devils in disguise, and once their fruit was tasted—never let their victims go.

But Mother and Aunt Lizzie had been released, their home protected...

Silence weighed upon Esther, suffocating her. She fled her room like a frightened creature, heedless of the fact that she wore no slippers, no dressing gown over her shift, her golden curls disheveled and unpresentable.

Esther reached her mother's room and halted, though she

5

had joyously burst into this sanctuary of comfort and safety countless times before. She hesitated, her pulse racing inexplicably, gooseflesh rising along her forearms.

"You are acting an absolute blithering fool, Esther Elizabeth Morris," she scolded herself, straightening with renewed determination. "You are nineteen years old, not a babe. Mother slept late for once is all."

Gritting her teeth and ignoring her shaking legs, Esther took a deep breath and opened the door, its hinges groaning.

She stilled at the sight that met her. God was not before her, but the devil's abhorrent carnage greeted her. Esther's mind simply ceased, unable to comprehend, lest her heart decline to beat a minute longer.

Lain across the bed, on sheets of blood-soaked crimson, was the horror that remained of her mother: her body shriveled and decayed far beyond its years; her eyes seared from her silver-haired head as if by burning pokers; her mouth opened wide in a silent scream.

The creak of a door filled the silence, and Esther still couldn't find the words to speak as her sister stepped into the hallway, rubbing her eyes, her own golden curls wild with sleep.

"Good morning," Kitty said cheerfully, yawning.

Esther yearned to slam the door in Kitty's face, to shield her sister from the fearful sight within. Yet her legs wouldn't obey her command, and her body stood frozen in place, her mind consumed by terror. Helpless, she watched like a mute stone as Kitty slipped into the room.

"Oh, what splendidly beautiful fruit, Mother!" Kitty exclaimed, smiling in delight, oblivious to what horror lay upon the bed mere feet from her.

Esther noticed for the first time what would have caught her own attention entirely had she only looked there first.

A shining golden platter of exquisite craftsmanship sat piled high with fruit of such decadence it nearly took Esther's breath away. Plump grapes—fresh from the vine—apricots and strawberries, twice the size of any she had ever seen, stacked upon lemons, oranges, apples, quinces, downy peaches, and plump pears. The cherries and raspberries, like jewels of summer, shone in the morning's light. Such perfection, all of it called to be tasted. Nothing this divine existed in her world, and she knew without a doubt that it had come from another.

Goblin fruit.

The lush scent grew bolder, masking the smell of her mother's blood.

Esther's legs obeyed her at last, and she rushed across the room. She knocked aside a rosy-skinned guava just as it nearly touched her sister's lips.

"The g-goblins," Esther stuttered, hardly believing herself, even as she spoke the undeniable truth.

Kitty's deep brown eyes widened in bewilderment.

"They did this to Mother."

Kitty paled. "Did what?"

Taking her sister firmly by the shoulders, Esther turned Kitty toward the bed, forcing her to keep her gaze trained upon their mother's withered and destroyed body.

"The goblins came at last for their revenge," Esther breathed. "Mother didn't escape after all."

Instead of screaming, Kitty walked to her mother's side, as if unsure of what rested before her. "This isn't real," she murmured, shaking her head. "I'm dreaming. I have to be dreaming..."

Though she was only a year younger than Esther, in that moment Kitty seemed like a child.

Their mother had taught them from an early age how to protect the house against goblins. The wards should have worked, so how had the creatures entered the house? Esther moved to their mother's windowsill to check her safeguards. The wards against the devilish creatures remained in place, but upon closer inspection, they were faded. The salts had turned gray. The garlic shriveled. The iron sword above her mother's bed was tinged in white, as if covered in frost. Searching the entire room, Esther saw a log in the fire, hollowed by flames, left with the remains of strange carvings amid the charred bark. She crept closer to the hearth, examining the markings. Her aunt had spoken of this technique only once, and even then, it had been a hushed and hurried conversation. One her mother hadn't taken all that seriously. But this was how the goblins had done it. Carvings inside the logs stayed hidden until, inevitably, they were used on a cold day. These stronger spells would counter all the worn-out forms of protection her mother and aunt had insisted upon.

"This is no dream," Esther said softly. "I wish that it were."

Kitty's body trembled, her chest heaving as tears streamed down her cheeks. Her sister grasped their mother's dead hand, squeezing it until her knuckles turned white.

"Wake," she begged.

But their mother would never wake again. Her body was destroyed, her heart ceased to beat, and there was no breath left in her lungs. With a sob, Kitty fled the room, Esther close behind her, down the hall and into the garden. The birds' usual calls were silent, as if all the world were in mourning, and there, Kitty flung herself onto a bench, inconsolable.

"I thought," Kitty whispered finally, her gaze fixed upon a crumpled dandelion. "I thought Mother had won."

Esther had always thought the same. Now, she knew they'd both been wrong. She wished she had paid more attention, asked more questions of her mother. Esther wrapped Kitty in her arms and held her close, rocking her gently until a horrid thought struck her.

"We must go to Aunt Lizzie," Esther said, pulling Kitty to her feet. "Make haste, sister, she could be in danger."

They ran to their aunt's house, hoping against hope that they would find her well. Esther knew their prayers were in vain as they grew near Aunt Lizzie's cottage. It fared worse than their own. Every rose, every vine of ivy, every oak tree, every yew and birch stood rotted and dead. Even the ground itself was decayed to dry and barren earth. And just the same as their house, the silence was deafening, the air impossibly still.

Trembling, the sisters entered the cottage. Their footsteps slapped the stone floor like claps of thunder while they traversed the hallway to their aunt's bedroom. And there upon the bed lay Aunt Lizzie, mutilated beyond recognition. Her eyeless head cradled in her withered arms, silver hair spilling along her blood-soaked dressing gown.

Only one thing in the room held any life.

Vibrant fruit was piled high upon a golden platter. The goblins' gift, or curse, shone in the morning sun, as if smiling in wicked triumph at them.

Three

KITTY

Their evil fruit, once tasted, is never forgotten. The vicar's words repeated in Kitty's mind, over and over again. The realization that once the goblins' magical fruit was tasted, the *maiden* was never forgotten struck her with renewed horror. The goblins had never forgotten the maidens who'd escaped them. They had made certain of their punishment.

Kitty wished with her entire heart that the goblins were only a superstitious legend, a reason to keep away from untoward men, a reminder to be cautious of strangers. But they weren't.

Their mother and aunt's triumph hadn't been a triumph at all. Their tragic ending yet to come, their tale incomplete, when they'd told Kitty and Esther of their time with goblins. No. The devious creatures had not forgotten the girls who had escaped them all those years ago. They had waited patiently, predators stalking their prey, until they found their way into the sisters' homes, stolen the breath from their lungs, the youth from their flesh, and spilled their blood in the most gruesome of ways. A sort of vengeance bestowed upon the sisters, proving a goblin never loses.

And a goblin never forgets.

"What do we do now, Esther?" Kitty sobbed in her sister's arms as the two sat in what remained of Aunt Lizzie's garden. Nothing but death and decay surrounded them.

Kitty's chest ached, her heart cracking as the images of her mother and aunt's bodies replayed in her mind's eye. Withered, bloody, all life *gone.*

Esther's lips pinched. The skin around her blue eyes was puffy, and pink splotches marked her cheeks from crying while she held onto Kitty. "We burn the fruit to make certain no one else is harmed by it, and we give our family proper burials."

Kitty nodded, wiping the tears from her own cheeks. The sisters were truly alone in this world.

Neither wanted to reenter the rooms in which their beloved mother and aunt lay, nor could they let the other go alone. Kitty's gaze drifted throughout the space, to the shadows, imagining goblins lingering there. The creatures watched her, mocking her fear, waiting in tickled anticipation for their next victims.

Yet there was no one there. Only the dead, and the deafening silence that replaced her mother and aunt's laughter.

Kitty held back a choked sob while lifting the golden platter of fruit, averting her gaze from her aunt who remained an empty shell. Yet she couldn't stop herself from stealing a glance at the enticing fruit. Even though she hadn't tasted it, she had touched one piece, and Kitty thought that it was perhaps enough for its evil to tempt her heart.

One taste, the fruit seemed to whisper. *Run your tongue*

against our skin, pierce our flesh with your teeth, taste our sweet juice. You know you want to...

Kitty resisted the urge to obey. She had but to recall the destroyed bodies of her beloved mother and aunt to turn temptation to hatred. This was what the sinister creatures were capable of, what they had done to her family.

What they would pay for if there was any justice in this world.

The two sisters returned home, encountering no one in the morning's thick fog. Then, after collecting the second golden platter, Kitty and Esther hid them carefully beneath their cloaks as they ventured into the field behind their home.

Securing the platters within the undergrowth of trees, they gathered kindling and built a fire. Wearing gloves, they tossed the fruit into the raging flames, waiting for its heat to swallow the poisonous and beautiful harvest, taking temptation with it. The alluring sugary-sweet scents of broiled strawberries, baking apples, and brûléed pears filled the air, and Kitty held her breath against it, though she yearned to reach into the fire and save just one piece.

Esther grasped Kitty's hand tightly. "I feel it too, Kitty. Don't give in to temptation. We must remain strong."

Kitty gritted her teeth and nodded, tears stinging her eyes once more. "What if resistance will be harder for us? Mother tasted the fruit—what if the poison's effects were passed down to us?"

Esther wrapped her arm around Kitty, holding her tightly as they wept. "Then we remain strong. We must promise to run away from the goblin market if we ever come across it and never look back."

When the pyre flared bright, its flames engulfing the fruit, the sisters dared to hope. But as the blaze died down to charcoal and ash, to their dismay, the goblins' evil gifts remained, just as whole and plump with life as before, the golden platters unmarred and shining.

"The fruit doesn't burn," Kitty whispered. "How is that possible?"

Esther stared at the remains before them. "We can't bury it since the fruit could possibly infect the ground and destroy our food and water supply. That leaves us no choice but to lock it away in the cellar where no one will ever find it."

WITH THE FRUIT HIDDEN IN THE BOTTOM OF A trunk and stored behind everything they could spare that would fit in their cellar, Kitty and Esther called upon Duncan to help them bury their mother and aunt.

Duncan ran his hand through his mussed hair, his face pale with concern. "You two can't remain here," he said.

"We'll get by, Duncan," Esther promised, her voice wavering. "We know how to take care of one another. Neither of us have tasted the goblin fruit, and we never will. You can rest assured of that."

"But—"

"Just please help us dig, Duncan. Our mother and aunt deserve that much before the entire village finds out what happened to them. They would never want the town to see them this way."

Kitty took a deep swallow. "Please, Duncan."

With a heavy sigh, he picked up the shovel and helped them dig their loved ones' graves. He then stood in silence as Esther said a prayer, Kitty's sobs accompanying her words.

After the funeral, they gathered the bloodied sheets from the rooms and placed them into a crackling bonfire.

As the sun set, it was time for Duncan to leave. "My parents have a spare room if you change your mind," he said.

Kitty could only look at the blood of her mother and aunt staining her dirt-covered hands.

"Thank you for your kindness." Esther shook her head. "But no, we won't be a burden on anyone."

Without another word, Duncan left, continuing to glance back at them until he walked out of sight.

The sisters stood over their mother and aunt's graves in silence, Kitty's heart withering, until the night sky hovered above them. She stared up at the star-filled night.

Why would you let this happen? she asked God. Yet she received no answer.

Esther led them inside, where they washed and scrubbed their skin until it was red and raw before finally retiring together in Esther's room. Their old wards remained, but if the goblins returned, would it matter?

Once Esther fell asleep, Kitty adjusted the blanket to cover her sister fully. Then she crept down to the cellar to find a bottle of her father's gin she knew her mother had kept, after he'd died, and brought out for rare occasions. It didn't matter now—her parents were both gone. There would be no more special occasions, would there?

Kitty avoided looking at the hidden trunk of fruit and hurried back to her sister's room. She drank, a bit too fast, but it didn't matter. Nothing mattered. All she wanted was to forget, forget the slain bodies of the women she loved, the images of which she saw every time she closed her eyes, the whole world going blood-red.

Nothing stayed a secret for long in the village, and Kitty

had no doubt that by morning everyone would know of what had happened. The next time she went to church, the sermon warning young maidens of the evil of goblins would include their mother and aunt's tragic end. That day, Kitty would be ill. She would make some excuse to avoid the vicarage for the foreseeable future.

Kitty drank until she couldn't anymore, then set the bottle roughly on the bedside table. *Ker-clunk.*

"Do you want to talk about it?" Esther asked, her eyes still red-rimmed and puffy from weeping.

"I'm frightened," Kitty slurred. "Frightened that you'll be taken too."

"Never. We stick together." Esther sat up and folded her arms around Kitty. "We fight together."

"Always." Kitty's stomach churned and she ran to the kitchen as nausea seeped up her throat.

Esther held back Kitty's hair while she continued to be sick into the steel bucket normally used for the hens' feed. As the room spun, Esther helped her into her room, and for the first time since they were little, they slept in the same bed, each protected by the other.

DAYS AND NIGHTS PASSED, AND KITTY FOUND THAT she couldn't fall asleep as easily as her sister. Esther seemed to simply slip into sweet oblivion, leaving Kitty to stare at the window of their now-shared room, wondering, always wondering if tonight the goblins would return.

But night after night, they didn't. Not even to collect their precious fruit down in the cellar.

Kitty couldn't stop herself from wishing she could hear

her mother's loving encouragement, her words of kind wisdom. She couldn't stop herself from missing how each morning there would be a bowl of fruit and eggs awaiting her. Now, the table was empty, the kitchen silent.

Each night she prayed to God to allow her to speak to her mother, to have one more moment with her, a final embrace that would allow her to move on, to live again. The gin helped her eventually fall asleep, to not wake in fear, and even though she knew her sister didn't approve, not once did Esther tell Kitty to put down the bottle.

Esther, in her turn, poured all her energy into their mother and Aunt Lizzie's bakery. She kept the house spotless, doing anything to distract herself from her loss. Customers didn't come as much anymore, perhaps afraid for their own lives should they associate too closely with the sisters, seeming to believe the goblins' evil magic was a contagious curse. The few new customers who did stop in, came as one might go to a circus to gawk at freaks, their morbid curiosity piqued.

"I hate the goblins with all my soul," Kitty said through gritted teeth as she placed a pie into the oven. Esther had told her not to think of the creatures, let alone speak of them. For all they knew, it could lure the goblins closer. However, as the days passed, Kitty decided that was precisely what she wanted, though she kept this to herself. She wasn't foolish enough to believe she could set things right if she came across the goblin market, yet maybe she could find some answers. Some way to make sense of her misery. She could be the one to figure out why the goblins did what they did at all. Why they had waited so long for their revenge. Why they couldn't simply let her mother and aunt live out their humble lives in peace. Why?

"Always beware the market," Aunt Lizzie had told her many times. "Once the goblins have a maiden in their clutches, they will not easily let her go."

"What about you and Mother? You two escaped them," Kitty had asked skeptically.

"Something that might never occur again." Aunt Lizzie had pursed her lips—fear blazed within the depths of her eyes.

Kitty's throat turned dry, and she reached for the gin on the counter behind her, drinking several long swigs.

All Kitty wanted was to see her mother again.

"Stop it," she ground out, wiping tears from her cheeks.

"Kitty," Esther called from the bakery's front.

"One moment!" Kitty answered. She brushed her hands down the front of her apron and met her sister. "Here I am."

Esther combed her fingers through her long golden hair, seemingly too distracted to notice Kitty's sadness. "I need to start on the cobblers, but we just got an order for five apple pies. I'm about ten apples short and was wondering if you'd be a darling and run to the market for me?"

Kitty smiled. "I could use some fresh air."

"And you know I prefer to be cooped up in here." Esther grasped Kitty's hand and squeezed it gently. "Get yourself something special while you're there. Perhaps a new journal? We've done decently the past few days."

Kitty nodded. Her sister hadn't missed the way she would write in her journal each night before bedtime, secretly penning letters to her mother and aunt that they would never read.

She collected her satchel and the gin, along with a wicker basket, then embraced her sister and kissed her cheek. Proper goodbyes were something Kitty had begun doing ever since that dreadful morning. If she could only clasp her mother and Aunt Lizzie in her arms again, she would never miss an opportunity to do so for the rest of her life.

"See you soon," she said softly. "I love you, Esther."

"I love you, too, Kitty." Esther smiled reassuringly as she dislodged herself from Kitty's embrace, though her eyes shone with tears. "Neither one of us is dying today. I promise. Now hurry back with my apples."

Outside, the sun shone across the narrow street. Hundreds of flowers decorated the florist's windows and shopfront, but Kitty couldn't admire their beauty, not when so much vibrant life only reminded her of her aunt's dead garden. And then there were the goblin wards, the hanging iron nails clinking against the door as the wind blew—a grim chime to her ears.

Her fingers itched for the gin bottle inside her satchel. Soon she would have to fight these urges, but not now. She took out the bottle, then downed half its contents, sighing at the rich juniper flavor that drifted down her throat and lingered on her tongue while soothing her wretched thoughts.

Duncan's fruit stand was only a few narrow lanes away, and already the stalls of the village square bustled with customers. The savory aroma of beef pasties permeated the air, and Kitty's stomach growled to consume it all. The world around her spun from the gin, her sorrow replaced with dizzying contentment.

As she passed by each booth, Kitty surveyed what they had to offer and decided against a journal for herself. Instead, she made up her mind to bring back something special for Esther.

"Good afternoon, Kitty. I haven't seen you in a while."

Duncan placed his hands on the table of his fruit stand, his face growing concerned. His auburn hair was drawn back into a low ponytail and his freckles were like constellations that she yearned to trace. No hint of judgement or fear shone in his mossy green eyes, even though he'd seen what the goblins could do, what they had *done*.

"Do you miss me?" Kitty slurred, stepping closer to him. "Perhaps you can come over tonight?"

"Kitty..." Duncan's throat bobbed.

Just as she was about to respond, a sweep of blonde hair darted between two trees in the distance. Kitty froze. She blinked, finding no one there. *Foolish girl.*

"Forgive me, Duncan. T-ten apples," Kitty stuttered, scanning the rest of the fruit. She pointed at one of the prizes she would give to her sister. "Oh, and that plum in the corner."

Duncan filled her basket, then handed her a few coins in change, and her heart skipped a beat. She hurried to tamp down her thoughts of how handsome he was.

"Let me walk you to the bakery when you finish?" he asked.

"*Fine.*" Kitty knew he was only being a gentleman, and if she were being truthful, she wouldn't mind him walking her back.

Wandering farther from Duncan's booth, she slowed to a stop near a wagon selling necklaces with different colored crystals dangling from silver and gold chains. She was about to ask for a sapphire one she knew Esther would adore when a flash of golden curls caught her eye again and Kitty gasped, forgetting everything at once. This time she wasn't imagining it, and she knew it wasn't the gin making her see things either. No one in the village had those wild curls except for her mother and aunt.

Kitty hurried to follow them, racing along the village road until she ended up at the edge of the forest, green foliage like emeralds beneath the sun. Her heart pounded, and she prayed with all her might that what she'd caught a glimpse of had not been a hallucination.

Kitty craned her neck and stood on her toes, peering between the tree trunks. Though she felt foolish to do it, she called, "Mother?"

She took out the bottle of gin once more, drinking every last sip as she waited for a response. Perhaps God had seen fit to finally answer her prayers, or perhaps the angels were blessing Kitty with a glimpse of her mother, to let her know she was safe.

As Kitty stumbled toward the forest, the impossible happened. Her mother stepped from behind an old yew tree, and the empty gin bottle slipped from Kitty's grasp. She looked just the same as she always had, only more radiant in a draping gown of silver silk. Ornate embroidery encircled her waist and decorated the hem.

"Mother!" Kitty's voice sounded like a plea, begging God not to take her away again. "Is it really you?"

"I heard your call, my sweet." Gliding forward, her mother wrapped her arms around Kitty, and she smelled just the same, of lavender and vanilla. "You've been praying every night, haven't you? Oh, Kitty, my darling, I've missed you. I want to show you my world. If you'll let me?"

Kitty trembled as she held her mother tighter. Her body swayed, her words slurring more than they had earlier. "I've missed you more than you can imagine. I've been searching for the goblin market, though I haven't told Esther."

"You must not ever search for it again." Her mother's gaze held the same stern rebuke it had when she'd told them her goblin story, the face that always made the sisters listen. "Promise me, Kitty. If you want to protect Esther, you mustn't." She placed a finger over Kitty's mouth before she could speak. "There's another reason I'm here. The heavens have blessed me with their celestial fruit. Fruit that will protect you and your sister from evil."

Kitty frowned, wondering if she'd heard her correctly. "Fruit?"

"Magical fruit, yes." Her mother held a pomegranate in her palm, and when Kitty looked at it, the fruit broke open, a shimmering geode in the afternoon sunlight. "Just one taste will keep you safe," she said softly. "Then we'll share it with your sister, and there will be nothing more to fear."

Kitty stared at the seeds, the red juice coating each of them like faceted rubies, and temptation swam within her gut. She wanted to eat not just one piece, but all of it. As the pomegranate's sweet and tart aroma enveloped her, Kitty could no longer hold back her desire, and eagerly, she dipped her fingers inside, then placed one aril on her tongue.

Whispers poured out around her, yet Kitty didn't see anyone else. She didn't care, not when faced with something so delicious as this magical fruit. She wanted nothing but to taste *more*.

Kitty moaned, her eyes fluttering closed—the world around her forgotten. Only she and this beautiful fruit existed. Grasping the pomegranate, Kitty ate and ate, stuffing her mouth as juice dribbled down her chin and stained her hands and the front of her dress like sticky blood—until there was nothing left.

She opened her eyes, licking the sweet red juice from her fingertips.

"A pity," her mother drawled. "Now we'll need another for your sister. In the meantime, how about you come along with me now? I have so many more wonders to show you."

"Oh yes," Kitty sang, clasping her hands together. The forest around her had brightened, the darkness inside her mind unfurling into colorful thoughts.

Silver wings fluttered above her, and at first Kitty believed them to be moths or butterflies, but when she looked more closely, she gasped. They were sprites just like from the fairy-tales she loved to read with Esther when they were children. They flew around Kitty in a fit of musical giggles, tucking white and purple flowers into her hair.

"Wait... Esther," Kitty said, massaging her temple.

But her mother cried, "We have to hurry!" She grasped Kitty's wrist, pulling her deeper into the forest. The trees were made of jewels, dew flickering like diamonds on their leaves, and Kitty wondered how she'd never noticed such beauty before.

Together, they ran, the forest blurring around them. Their feet moved as if on clouds, until at last they broke through the trees and Kitty halted, her lips parting in awe.

Before her stood a castle of glass and gold. A golden drawbridge beckoned to her, ivory swans swimming beneath it amongst the lily pads, lotus petals in mauve, bright against their snowy feathers.

"Is this Heaven?" Kitty asked, breathless.

Her mother smiled wide. "This is a magical kingdom, where no one ever grieves."

Kitty gawked in wonder, each sight more fantastical than the last.

"I have another secret, my beautiful child. The king has been waiting for you."

"The king? Waiting for me? Surely, he doesn't want to meet..."

Who was Kitty thinking about? She lost her train of thought as she followed her mother toward the palace doors. Gardens beyond her imagination spread out across sloping grounds. Purple roses, the size of cakes, glowed like amethysts. Honeysuckle, orchids, and birds of paradise swooped over sparkling fountains in the warm sunlight.

Two male guards wearing gold and white uniforms drew a set of towering doors open, and an enchanting melody poured out. The music, a blend of cello, harp, and piano, enveloped Kitty and tugged her forward as if by her heartstring. As she passed one of the guards, the freckles on his face reminded her of someone...a boy selling fruit at the market... Who was he again? The music grew distorted as she tried to think. *Think...*

"Come on, darling," her mother said.

Kitty blinked and shook her head, finding the music lovely once more as she focused on following her mother.

Suddenly, she stood in a room filled with faces. All of them smiled radiantly at her. Kitty peered around the room, halting on an ornate mirror hanging on the wall where the image reflected back at her was different. The people's eyes were hollow, their grins sinister. Her pulse quickened as a sinking feeling gripped her. But when she whirled around, welcoming expressions greeted her. It had only been her imagination.

Bowing their heads, the crowd stepped aside to reveal her aunt, dressed in a pale velvet gown, her hair plaited down her back. Kitty stilled, believing it wasn't real, but it was, and she rushed forward with an ecstatic cry.

"I'm elated you're here." Aunt Lizzie enfolded Kitty in her arms, and happiness consumed her. *Happiness.* "King Errol awaits you, dear niece."

The crowd parted once again, and a man of striking beauty stepped forward. A golden crown sat atop his head, his obsidian hair falling in silken sheets down his back. Eyes of sapphires met hers, so blue and so perfect that she couldn't cast her gaze away from his. This was the man she'd always known would court her. It was laughable that she'd ever thought of another man at all. There had never, *could* never be any other.

"At last we meet, enchanting Kitty. I've been waiting such a long time." He held his hand out to her, and Kitty grasped it, his touch sending a comforting warmth through her.

She blinked, and a smile matching everyone's in the room spread across her face. "I've been waiting for you, too."

"You are forever protected from harm here, my love." He tucked a lock of hair behind her ear, his smile like a thousand suns. And then King Errol knelt, his sapphire eyes on hers, pleading devotion everlasting, taking her heart all at once. The entire court seemed to hold their breath in anticipation. "I have something to ask of you."

"What is it?"

"Dearest Kitty, will you do me the honor of being my queen?"

"Yes," she whispered, forgetting—forsaking—the world she'd left behind. "Yes, I will."

Four

ESTHER

Esther finished placing two gooseberry pies in their boxes before bringing them out to Mrs. Lofton, a half-blind elderly woman who came in once a week for the same purchase. She handed Mrs. Lofton the desserts and accepted her coin absently, peering out the window as rain began to pour from the sky. Anxiety washed over her—why hadn't Kitty returned yet? Ever since the murders, Esther had been overstressed, hesitant to leave her sister alone. Perhaps she should've just gone to the market with her. But she couldn't watch over Kitty like her shadow forever.

Just when Esther was sure she would go mad with worry, the door burst open, and Duncan stumbled into the bakery with Kitty in his arms, drenched to the bone and shivering. The basket of apples spilled from her hands, and Kitty nearly collapsed to the floor in a fit of laughter. Mrs. Lofton startled, clutching her cross, and Esther hurried past the woman to aid her sister.

"Dreadfully sorry, Mrs. Lofton," Esther apologized.

"Kitty isn't feeling well, and I need to close the shop. I'm sure you understand."

"Of course." Yet Mrs. Lofton's face had paled, and she rushed out of the store as if she believed a curse would fall upon her. Esther hoped she would return—they needed her weekly purchases.

"Thank you for helping her," she said to Duncan, then turned to snap at Kitty as the overwhelming reek of alcohol invaded Esther's senses. "Did you drink too much gin at the market? Couldn't you have waited until we returned home?"

But Kitty only continued to laugh and shiver in Duncan's arms.

Esther turned to Duncan. "Will you help me get her home?"

"Of course," he said, looking uncomfortable with the situation. Nevertheless, he adjusted Kitty in his arms. She turned her head into his chest and closed her eyes with a sigh.

Esther locked the bakery, and they hurried home through the pouring rain. Once inside the warm cottage, she guided Duncan to the bedroom where he laid Kitty gently on the bed, blushing furiously. Esther thanked him again, and he hurried to leave, apologizing all the while.

The sisters now alone, Esther attempted to unfasten the back of Kitty's soaked dress.

"No, I like my dress," Kitty sang. "It's a glorious dress! Fit for a queen, this dress is."

"You'll make yourself sick!" Esther scolded, reaching for the button again. This time Kitty stood still, allowing Esther to remove her wet clothing and dress her in a dry nightgown.

Kitty didn't utter another word, only fell into their bed and shut her eyes. Her breaths came short and shallow. Esther sighed and sat beside her sister on the bed, bringing the blankets up to cover Kitty's shoulders. She noticed her sister's flushed cheeks and placed her hand to Kitty's forehead, finding her skin hot. Esther scrambled for a cloth and some cool water, then placed the rag to Kitty's forehead.

Esther stayed by her sister's side throughout the night, barely getting a wink of sleep, and this continued for the next two days, as Kitty's health continued in much the same way. She slept restlessly, hardly eating and drinking very little water. Esther's chest remained tight, the worry not letting up.

"No doctor," Kitty moaned for the twentieth time on the third day of her illness, her eyelids fluttering. "I'm *fine*. Honestly."

"If you aren't improved by midday, I'm calling on the physician," Esther promised.

But soon enough Kitty slept soundly. Her color so much improved as the day went on, Esther didn't have the heart to disturb her.

THE NEXT MORNING, ESTHER LONGED TO REMAIN beneath the warmth of her quilts. Ever since her mother and aunt's deaths, warding the house more than her family ever had, handling the bakery, taking care of Kitty's illness, Esther felt as if she'd barely had time to breathe. The weather had been especially miserable the past few days. A frigid mist clung to mud-caked lanes, an unrelenting icy downpour from a bruised sky. It was as if everything in the world were in mourning, the country turned wilted and forlorn.

Esther struggled to summon the courage to leave her warm bed, when someone knocked on the door.

Had she slept past the hour of the flour delivery?

No, today was Tuesday. Flour was always delivered on Thursdays. To the bakery, not the house. Perhaps it was Duncan checking to make certain they were all right. She glanced at Kitty, only to find her already up, which pleased her.

"Kitty, are you answering that?" Esther shouted, but her sister didn't reply.

Esther pushed aside the quilt and left her bed with a sigh of irritation, toes desperately searching for slippers lest her feet touch the frosty floorboards. She shrugged into her woolen dressing gown as the knocking persisted.

"One moment, please!" she called, hurrying down the hallway, attempting to straighten her hair.

"Yes, yes, *what*? Who is it?"

But no one stood outside the cottage door. Only rain and fog met Esther's gaze—the grass next to the brick path had turned to a muddy pond beneath the weeping willow.

The knocking continued, startling Esther, and she spun, gazing at the hallway with sudden fear. The sound came from within the house.

Kitty.

The knocking grew louder as Esther ran back down the hall, her heart pounding in time with the sound, her blood going cold. She would never forgive herself if anything happened to Kitty, never.

The noise echoed from their mother's room.

"Kitty?" Horror coursed through Esther's veins as she opened the door. "Are you—"

Kitty faced the room's shadowy corner, her arms hanging slack at her sides. Her nightgown was torn, her feet bare, and her hair a nest of tangles. Kitty smashed her forehead against the wall, again and again.

Knock. Knock. Knock.

"*Kitty!*" Esther rushed to her sister, throwing her arms around her, and pulled her away from the blood-splattered wall. Blood fell like black tears from her sister's face, splattering ruby red onto her pale toes. "What's happened? Please..."

Why hadn't she insisted upon the physician immediately?

"So beautiful," Kitty whispered, her eyes staring blankly. "I'm so hungry, Esther. So hungry... Why am I still hungry? I've eaten so much already."

"Shh," Esther pleaded, guiding Kitty back into her room. She helped her toward the bed. "Lie down. I'll fetch you something to eat."

"Some grapes would be lovely, Esther, thank you."

Grapes...

Esther's thoughts flew to the dreaded fruit hidden deep within their cellar, but when she fled downstairs to check, it was all still there. She should've known Kitty wouldn't have been foolish enough to taste it. But there was no denying that Kitty exhibited the symptoms of consuming their fruit, symptoms that Esther knew from her mother and Aunt Lizzie's stories.

With Kitty beneath her quilts at last, Esther hurried to dress, and, feeling the two of them were left more alone than ever, she did the last thing in the world she wanted to do. Though she had no choice, she abandoned Kitty with no one to watch over her.

The village's only physician, a Doctor Evans, was an old man of hairy ears and poor eyesight. A man not too pleased about being woken by a hysterical young woman first thing in the morning and even less pleased to be asked to go out in the rain.

He took his time muttering about a carriage and would have eaten a hot breakfast had not Esther nearly screamed at him in her agitation.

"After all, Doctor, it's only six doors down from here," Esther tried. "And you've known Kitty since the moment she was born. I'm fearful the goblins may have done something to her."

"Yes, yes, all right," Doctor Evans grunted, reluctantly following her into the rain. "But only because I know you two are alone after the..." He didn't finish the sentence, yet it wasn't hard to decipher his meaning.

Reaching the house, Esther nearly screamed again as the man took centuries to walk down the hall, and once he examined Kitty, her eyes continuing to stare blankly at the ceiling, he didn't seem half as alarmed as Esther felt he should've been, all things considered.

"Hmm, I don't believe this is goblins' work. Fever can present many psychological symptoms, you see," he told Esther calmly, unconcerned over the fact that Kitty's skull might have been fractured. Soaking cotton batting in carbolic acid, he placed it across Kitty's forehead to clean her wounds, and the sweet-smelling clear liquid nearly made Esther gag, while her sister made no sign that she noticed at all.

"But, Doctor, her *head*! Surely—"

"A woman, luckily, doesn't possess the strength for inflicting lasting damage to herself in that way," he said. "Not to worry, Esther, my dear. Not to worry."

Esther's agitation grew, her heart thudding. The man couldn't be serious.

"But what should we *do*, Doctor? Look at her, she's just...*lying* there with her eyes open as if..." All she could think about was her mother, slaughtered. Her aunt—bloody and broken. She couldn't lose Kitty as well. Her sister was all she had left, the one reason she got out of bed and went into the bakery to keep a roof over their heads.

"The other women who were lured in by goblins didn't appear to share these symptoms, no. Not in my experience, which I admit is not much, but there you have it. Fear not. All that is needed is some quinine and cool compresses against her neck and shoulders, which should have young Kitty back on her feet making Battenberg cakes in no time."

He handed Esther a bottle of the medicine, adding, "Morphine and arsenic, if need be, but it shouldn't be necessary." He closed his satchel with a final snap, smiling brightly as Kitty lay behind him like a corpse, and accepted ten shillings with hardly a glance. "Let me know if there's no change after two days."

And without another word, the physician was gone.

Esther decided to close the bakery until Kitty was well, hardly leaving her side for the rest of the day, changing her bandages, placing cold compresses against her skin. She sat with her until her eyes could no longer stay open and Esther's head fell against the bed, Kitty's cold hand in hers. Tears filling her eyes, she hummed an old song that their mother used to sing to them to make them feel better during an illness or a scrape. Esther had not prayed since the day her mother died, but she prayed then, prayed that Kitty was truly ill and that this wasn't the goblins' work.

When gray morning light seeped through the curtains once again, Esther jolted awake, her neck stiff, her blanket falling to the floor as she stood with a cry. Her lungs froze in her chest, and she could barely find the air to keep from fainting.

Doctor Evans could not have been more wrong—this was goblin fruit doing as she'd first feared.

Tears of rage and helplessness stung her eyes. She pinched herself, praying she would wake, but what rested before her was real.

Kitty lay against her pillows, now an old woman. Her golden curls turned to thin wisps of silver. Her colorless skin appeared as wrinkled and withered as melted wax. Her milky eyes were wide open, embedded in deep sockets. Her once full and rosy cheeks now sank around rotting teeth, and Kitty's beauty of just the day before had faded to someone unrecognizable.

Five

KITTY

itty watched with bated breath as the king rose to his feet in otherworldly glory. He crossed the room until his tall form hovered above her, his gaze full of longing. She was to be his partner, his *wife*.

"Now, my queen," Errol said, his sapphire eyes holding hers, his smile radiant. "In honor of the kingdom's new bride, we will observe thirteen days of celebration. Anything you desire or wish for will be granted."

He leaned in close, and the heady scent of apples enveloped Kitty, making her crave the fruit. His warm breath tickled her neck as he whispered, "You look absolutely stunning."

Kitty's heart leapt at Errol's closeness, sending heat straight into her blood. He stepped back and she looked down at herself, smiling in wonder. Her simple blue dress and worn boots transformed into delicate layers of ivory chiffon and pearl-embroidered lace that hugged her form, and as she lifted the gown's hem, Kitty found she wore crystal slippers that perfectly fit her feet. Gold embroidery of breathtaking craftsmanship embellished the gown's sleeves and skirt.

Kitty gasped. A golden tattoo of leaves and vines encircled her ring finger, its curves shining beneath the chandeliers. Her hair fell in thick curls to her waist instead of its usual plait—Kitty resisted the urge to twirl like a child.

"Behold all of your beauty, my love." The king lifted his hand and waved her mother toward them.

Her mother, smiling proudly, held a mirror. Its frame sparkled with silver fruit. Kitty blinked as she stared at her reflection, an image she couldn't believe was herself. A crown of golden leaves and vines, embedded with emeralds and diamonds, sat atop her head. Gloss stained her rosebud lips, and sparkling powders decorated her cheeks and deep brown eyes. Even her lashes appeared longer and thicker. Kitty never imagined she possessed such rare beauty, but in this moment, she found she was a match for any king.

"If only your sister were here to see you." Her mother sighed, her eyes brimming with tears.

"Yes, your sister," Aunt Lizzie added from behind her, sadness filling her gaze. "Her place is with us. The five of us together. One. Happy. Family."

"Yes, we would love to meet your sister," the crowd chanted in unison, each man and woman taking a step closer to Kitty, as if to embrace her.

If only Esther *were* here, Kitty knew her sister would absolutely adore the palace and the enchanting beauty surrounding it.

"Yes, Esther belongs here." Kitty beamed. "She must come at once!"

Errol gently lifted Kitty's chin, his apple-scented breath mingling with hers. She'd never felt a tenderness from a man like this before. "If that is what you wish, then your sister will join us. I'll make certain of it. She will have a room inside the palace, and you can appoint her any title you choose. How does that sound, my queen?"

Esther could have a title all her own, something prestigious she could be proud of. She would never have to worry about the bakery again, never have to concern herself with nosy customers, or earning enough to feed them and keep a roof over their heads. Most of all, Esther would be with her family, and that would make her the happiest sister in the world.

"That sounds wonderful," Kitty said. "Thank you, Your Majesty, for your kind generosity."

"What's mine is yours." Errol trailed his thumb across her lower lip, and Kitty's eyelids fluttered at his intoxicating touch. "And now, how about a dance, my love?"

"Yes." Her voice came out as a sigh.

Music filled the palace once more, and Kitty gasped to discover they stood in the center of a majestic ballroom of shining marble and gold beneath chandeliers holding hundreds of silvery candles. Violins accompanied the cellos and piano, the tempo picking up, and the dancers stepped forward. Dressed in the finest gowns and silks of every color, the entire court formed lines around their king and queen, the women across from the men. Errol stood before Kitty, his eyes hooded and his smile seductive as he bowed. Kitty curtsied, slow and provocative, smiling in return.

The king stepped forward to begin the dance. Their arms brushed, skin kissing skin, ever so briefly as they circled one another, mirroring each other's movements, their rhythms perfectly matched. Errol's smile widened, his gaze mischievous, and he wrapped his arm around Kitty's waist, pulling her close while they danced. Kitty couldn't help but succumb, dizzy with the melodious sounds that repleted her very soul. All around the ballroom, the other couples followed suit, perfectly mimicking Kitty and her king, as if the whole kingdom were one exquisite flower, blooming in silks, jewels, and lace.

While Kitty danced and danced, she noted the crowd's focus on her. Their wide, unmoving smiles stayed planted on their faces, their eyes unblinking. And though Kitty had never felt so merry in all her days, something dark brewed within her chest. She felt that everything was...

It was...

She could barely find the air to breathe, her lungs heaving, as shadows slithered across the faces of the crowd.

"Eat," the king purred, bringing a strawberry of shining ruby red to her lips.

That smell...that intoxicating and alluring smell. Kitty couldn't refuse the fruit's sweet temptation and took it between her teeth. A moan escaped her when its juices filled her mouth, pleasure bursting along her tongue and throat.

"More," she whispered, unable to remember why she'd been so nervous moments before.

"Anything you desire," Errol said softly, bringing another strawberry to her lips, then offered her a glass of raspberry wine. She sipped and it tasted of heaven.

Movement caught her attention, and Kitty gasped as butterflies of lustrous metallic colors fluttered beneath the domed ceiling. Sprites with iridescent wings, containing all the hues of the rainbow, came forth through the walls. They laughed in delight and tossed silver and white flowers upon the dancers. Velvety petals drifted down from their tiny fingers like snow.

The wedding was akin to a dream; one Kitty felt exuberant joy thinking she would never have to wake from, because this was all real. She'd always wanted a lavish wedding, yet with their family's modest income, she had never thought it possible. And even though she hadn't fully realized it until now, this king was who Kitty had always imagined being her husband, her true love. As warmth spread inside her, seeping lower and lower, she wanted desperately to leave this room and find a place where they could be alone.

Seeming to dip into her thoughts, Errol's fingertips skimmed down her spine and halted on her tailbone. "Should we make haste to our bedchamber or dance another round?" he drawled. "I'm desperate to taste your lips. To taste *all* of you."

Her mother and aunt watched from the edge of the crowd, nodding encouragement, as if they heard his words and read her thoughts.

"Yes," Kitty said, knowing that if she stayed in the ballroom a moment longer, she would kiss her king in front of everyone, regardless of how unladylike it might be.

Errol bit his lip as he smiled shyly. He then grasped her hand and twirled her past the dancing crowd before leading Kitty into the shadows of a winding staircase.

While he climbed the steps beside her, she couldn't resist sneaking glances at his elegance, his perfection. And he was *hers*.

At the top of the stairs, a long corridor of luxurious carpet in various shades of blue stretched out before them. Kitty's heart galloped at the sight of the wide golden doors at its end. Ornate panels cast in metal of gold, copper, and silver decorated the walls on either side of them. Warm flames in recessed sconces brought the carvings to life, guiding the newlyweds forward, the ballroom's music fading in the distance.

As they reached the hallway's end, Errol smiled, charming enough to make her knees weak. He reached for one of the curved handles made of crystal that matched her slippers and motioned her inside their bedchamber.

Kitty's breath caught as she gaped around the room in awe, taking in its alluring luxury. Never had she seen anything so lavish. Emerald silk pillows of every size and embroidered quilts covered the massive bed. Vines ran along the wooden canopy to yet more greenery decorating the molding of the ceiling, numerous flowers blooming from them. Paintings of mystical creatures hung on the iridescent walls in gilded frames.

A glass writing desk hugged one corner, and a wardrobe of the same material stationed across from the bed between towering windows. Another door led to what must be the bathing chamber, and the thought of them washing one another made Kitty's heart thunder exquisitely against her rib cage.

"Take a peek inside the wardrobe, my queen," Errol said as he studied her with open delight.

Kitty drew the doors wide and squealed in excitement. The wardrobe opened to a room the size of her entire house back home, its gilded walls brimming with gowns and shoes and hats of such beauty it made her head spin.

"Oh, Errol!" She whirled to face him. "This is magnificent."

He smiled, his eyes dancing with amusement. "More gifts are waiting for you on the desk. And more will come each day."

Kitty looked to the desk, and her lips parted when she

saw what he'd brought her. A golden platter filled with luscious fruit—grapes, oranges, berries, and pears—lay beside a jeweled goblet of wine.

Errol's lithe fingers plucked a berry from its twisted stem and placed it between her lips.

"Mm." She sighed, forgetting the world as its magical sweetness consumed her.

Errol chuckled, the sound deep and musical, while his arm circled her waist from behind to pull her against his strong body. She couldn't stop herself from arching into him, craving the feel of him.

"If you wish it, I can show you just how much I adore you, my darling Kitty." His lips trailed down the curve of her neck, his teeth grazing her skin, electrifying her entire being.

Kitty couldn't renounce the way she felt, couldn't renounce anything that could be had between them on this night.

"Please," she begged, turning in his arms to meet his gaze. She cupped Errol's cheeks and brought his face closer, then pressed her lips to his. Her first kiss. A kiss that would never be forgotten. The king tasted of the sweetest fruit, the magical and wonderful ripeness, which only made her yearn for his kisses more.

"So wild." Errol smiled against her lips. "Like an animal set free. I chose my queen rather well, did I not?" He broke their embrace to place their crowns on the desk before lifting Kitty into his arms. She wrapped her legs around his narrow hips, and he walked them to his bed.

Their lips coasted over one another's, desperate, the sweet taste of fruit on his tongue growing ever stronger, leaving Kitty wanting yet more. Errol sank on the mattress, Kitty in his lap, her legs cradling his thighs, and as she moved against him, she had only one thought. She wanted more. More. More. *More.*

"I've been saving myself for only you," she whispered, pulling the hem of his tunic free before lifting it over his head.

"A gift I could never refuse," Errol purred, unlacing the ties at the back of her gown until she sat bare before him. "So beautiful." he whispered, kissing her bare shoulder, his lips trailing starlight and butterflies along her skin as they traveled to her neck, then lower. "So inviting."

Soon, there was nothing left between them but skin, every curve and muscle begging to be touched.

Errol held her in his arms and lay them down on the silken quilt. "Moan," he said. "Say you're mine."

"I'm yours," Kitty gasped.

And then his lips were on hers once again, all-consuming, his flavor making her plead for more. His apple scent permeated the air, driving Kitty mad.

The king's kisses drifting to her neck, he inhaled deeply, and for a moment—just one—a wave of exhaustion crashed over Kitty, his scent of apples transforming to the stench of rotting fruit. Something tugged within her chest, as if her rib cage were being pulled forward.

Madness.

She was going *mad.* Imagining this world of wonder slipping...

As she parted her lips to voice her concerns, the king ran a juice-covered finger across her lips, and she sighed with contentment. Her perfect reality fell back into place, along with Errol's intoxicating scent, her fatigue vanished. She could only think of her king, her glorious Errol, with his magical fruit, fruit she could happily eat forever and never tire of its sweetness.

"And I am yours," Errol vowed. "I obey your will alone."

"Give me all of you," Kitty murmured. "As I give you all of me."

And as he did, Kitty swore the stars shone through the ceiling. She felt none of the pain she'd heard there would be when maidenhood was given. Only pleasure, undeniable pleasure and love as she held her husband in her arms, love that left all the romantic tales to pale in comparison. Kitty never wanted to leave this world, this palace, this bed, never wanted to leave Errol's arms.

Forever. And ever. And ever.

She and her king.

Eating and pleasuring.

Eating and pleasuring.

Eating and pleasuring.

Six

ESTHER

itty was unresponsive, no matter how hard Esther tried to rouse her. Her sister lay still, her milky eyes wide as she stared vacantly at the ceiling. It was as if Kitty were lost in a dream, unable to wake. Esther pressed her ear to Kitty's chest and could feel her sister's heart tripping along inside. Her wasted form as still as death, yet her heart still beat. She looked so old, so frail. All because of a goblin and its wicked fruit.

"Weeping will accomplish nothing," Esther told herself, wiping her tears with both hands, her determination to do something—*anything*—to save her sister overwhelming.

"What had Aunt Lizzie done when Mother seemed all but lost to her?" Esther asked, but Kitty made no reply. "Did she cry like a helpless babe? No, she did not. She searched for the goblin market herself. So, that's precisely what I must do now."

Esther had no idea where to begin—and no idea of what she might do if she did, by some miracle, find the creatures—

but remembering her mother's stories, Esther decided the river was the best place to start.

Yet how could she leave Kitty alone in her state? It was unthinkable. What if she were to hurt herself again? "I'll only be gone for a few moments," Esther promised and ran through the fog to Duncan's cottage.

She found him tending his vegetable garden in the weak sunlight and rushed forward. Duncan wiped his shirtsleeve across his dirt-smeared brow and paled when he spotted her. "What is it?" he asked in alarm, dropping the shovel to the ground.

"It's Kitty. I need you to look after her. Please, Duncan," Esther begged. "I would ask anyone else, but please understand, there is no one."

"I am at your service," Duncan said.

"And please don't tell anyone what you see there, for Kitty's sake."

"Anything. For Kitty's sake, of course." His throat bobbed and he nodded. "What do you need of me?"

"At the market, it wasn't only gin she consumed but also goblin fruit. Duncan, she's aged drastically." Esther held back a sob, struggling to pull herself together in the face of Duncan's sympathy. "I need to find something that will help Kitty. Anything."

Even if it meant finding a goblin the way her aunt once had.

"I didn't see anything out of the ordinary that day." He sighed, his hand running across his jaw. "No goblins, nor their market. Unless one had been lurking about in disguise..."

It was believed that goblins could disguise their form in

the human world in order to lure their victims, that one's eyes mustn't be trusted against them. Kitty had been in despair after the death of her mother, making her easy prey for the goblin's deception. "They know how to be tricky. That is for certain."

DUNCAN BURNED AWAY THE LAST OF THE CURSED wood in their mother's room while Esther busied herself decorating Kitty's surroundings with every talisman, charm, and superstitious nonsense against goblins she had ever learned. Opening the drapes, she allowed what light there was into the house, no matter how feeble its rays. To this, Esther added as many candles as they could spare until the room was brighter than a summer afternoon. Next, she hung glass bottles in the window and doorway. Taking every crucifix from the house, she set them around Kitty, before adding fresh salt to the window ledge and door. Fetching garlic from the kitchen, Esther laid the braided bulbs around Kitty's still form like garland placed over the dead, then decorated her eyes with black soot from the kitchen fireplace. Iron, as much as she could find joined the mix, and then, after drawing the conjoined circles of the devil's shield against every mirror and windowpane with yet more soot, Esther rested their worn Bible against Kitty's chest.

"I need you to stay strong," Esther encouraged, trailing a hand down her sister's wrinkled cheek.

Kitty said nothing for a long moment until she startled Esther by exclaiming in regular tones, "Mother will bring her. Then we'll celebrate in full!"

Esther stared. Kitty displayed no change. Her eyes remained fixed on the ceiling above her, her form still as decrepit with supernatural age as before, and she made no struggle to be released from her bonds.

"Such a lovely gown!" Kitty shouted, then fell silent.

Esther's chest tightened. What were the goblins doing to her sister?

"Go," Duncan said, settling into a chair at Kitty's side. "I'll keep her safe."

There was precious little time to waste, and Esther trusted Duncan more than anyone else in the village. This would have to suffice. "Don't answer the door for anyone," she instructed.

Pressing her lips to Kitty's forehead, Esther sobbed and said, "Stay alive, sister. I promise..." But she didn't know what she promised. Regarding the pitiful state Kitty now found herself in, Esther knew she had no right to promise her sister anything ever again.

Wiping her tears, Esther gathered her overcoat and one of her father's small old blades before leaving her home. The morning was miserably cold, a light rain spitting down through fog thick as smoke. She wasted no time, fleeing past cottages looking forlorn in the midday gloom. Esther barely spared a glance at her closed bakery, hurrying through the still-deserted village square, past the tavern and its stables, until she reached the forest lane, paying no mind when a passing carriage splattered her skirts with mud.

Somehow she would find the goblins and barter her life for her sister's if that was what it came down to.

But Esther searched in vain. Wandering along the riverbank most of the day, she found nothing more than broken bottles and the discarded remains of cigarettes. As Esther trudged back toward her home to check on her sister, a high-pitched voice shouted her name near the bakery. Winifred, Esther's dear old pen friend, stood at its door, hat in hand.

"Esther!" she cried, rushing forward. "Oh, Esther, I came as soon as I heard of your tragedy. I went to the house hours ago, but no one answered, so I came here."

Esther thought of Kitty, knowing there wasn't time to waste.

"I'm so sorry, Winifred. I know you came all this way, but the goblins got to Kitty, and I don't know how much longer she will endure their poison," Esther sobbed. Even though she hadn't seen Winifred in a year, they'd never stopped writing letters to one another.

"The goblins!" Winifred hissed, showcasing her front tooth that had nearly rotted away.

At this, Esther could no longer hold back her tears. Falling into Winifred's embrace, she told her all that had happened from the morning she woke and found her mother dead. Everything, except the golden platters of fruit and where they now lay hidden. That was a secret between her and Kitty, and something her dear friend wouldn't understand.

Winifred furrowed her brow. "My aunt once told me about an herbalist widow who is really a witch. You could—"

"A witch?" Esther perked up, hope coursing through her veins. Was there truly such a thing? All the herbalists she'd heard of were useless against the goblin fruit.

Winifred nodded. "It's rumored she's helped many with spells. They say she could cure the devil himself." She glanced at her pocket watch. "Oh dear, I would stay for an entire fortnight if I could, but the truth is, the factory never tolerates absence. We can't afford to lose even the price of my train ticket, let alone my place at the factory."

"Will you at least tell me how to find her?" Esther's feet itched to move, to find an answer. There was yet light in the sky. If the witch lived close by, she could reach her before dark and return home in time to force something into Kitty's mouth, water at the very least.

Winifred tucked her watch back inside her coat. "Oh, finding her is simple. Follow the lane behind the chapel that leads into the northern forest, and you will soon see her cottage."

Esther embraced her friend. "Thank you."

"Take care, my dear Esther," she called as Esther took off running. "I will keep you and Kitty in my prayers!"

Esther continued down a winding road until she stumbled upon the dirt lane behind the village chapel, though it was overgrown with weeds. Rain continued to pelt her face. A black cat stared at her with its eerie yellow eyes as she passed into the forest, and Esther shuddered, thinking again of witches. Though the sun hadn't yet set, the trees cast deep shadows over the misty undergrowth, and Esther wished she'd thought to bring a lantern with her. But just when she hesitated in her stride, beginning to turn back, the widow's cottage stood before her.

Moss-covered stone and gnarled wooden doors and windows, the home tilted, sinking into the damp earth beneath it. No smoke twirled from the chimney. And not a single speck of light shone from its windows, the glass black like a cluster of spider eyes. Panic traveled through Esther's veins; the place seemed abandoned.

Forgetting her fears of returning home in the dark, she rushed forward, skirts in hand, and knocked.

"Hello!" Esther shouted. "Is anyone there?"

"Yes, yes," a voice answered a moment later. "I'm old, not deaf. Go away."

Esther knocked again, this time waiting until the door opened before speaking and placing one foot firmly in the doorway. A plump woman with rosy cheeks and silver braids coiled neatly atop her head peered up at Esther from the shadows of the threshold. A clean, ruffle-edged apron protected her cheerful floral dress. She looked nothing like Esther's estimation of a witch.

"Well? What do you want?" she said finally. "I'm just a poor widow. I want no trouble."

"Please," Esther begged. "I'm sorry to bother you at this late hour, but my sister is very ill and needs help. She ate the goblins' fruit. I thought maybe—"

"Maybe I'm a *witch*, is that it?" The widow scowled, then suddenly burst into song, startling Esther. "Let me guess, a calamitous mess! You asked the doctor, and you asked the priest, and you asked *all* the village to grant you peace, but they gave you none, an ugly shun, you were undone! And so, at last the lass comes running, running, running to the witch, a last ditch, a pretty switch!" As she sang, the widow moved forward from the shadows, bobbing her head back and forth like a Punch and Judy puppet, and Esther stepped back in alarm. The woman was clearly not well.

But mad or not, if she could help Kitty...

"No, no," Esther tried, "not at all, I—"

"Well," the woman spoke in even tones again, shrugging dismissively as she turned back to the doorway. "I'm nothing but a poor widow who minds her own affairs and knits cardigans in exchange for scraps. Take your troubles elsewhere." She tapped her chin. "Unless," she cooed, "you can pay?"

Esther had two shillings in her pocket, and she readily handed them over to the widow, who snatched them up.

"I may know a thing or two about *special* herbal remedies, after all," she said. "Follow me. Don't stand outside in the cold like a lost kitten."

Esther hurried behind the widow, and even though the cottage had appeared dark from the outside, inside she found it well-lit with candles and a roaring fireplace. Every conceivable surface was decorated with knitted blankets, rugs, and tablecloths, giving the space a warm, calm atmosphere.

"Now," uttered the widow. "Tell me your troubles."

Esther took a deep breath and began, "After the goblins murdered our mother and aunt, they've—"

"So I've heard..." She pointed at a newspaper with one bony finger, and Esther read the headline: "Village Sisters Murdered by Goblins". "I have never known them to murder in such a vicious way. This is most unusual, yes..."

"It's because they survived the goblins' fruit long ago," Esther said with a frown.

The widow clucked her tongue. "Interesting."

"They're draining my sister's very soul as we speak," Esther cried. "Please, I need your help. Her youth has dwindled, and I don't know how much longer she'll have."

"I know just the thing, my dear," she drawled. "A draught that lets one enter another's consciousness."

"Is such a thing possible?"

"Why, of course it is!" the widow exclaimed. "It's simple as pie, only those idiotic doctors would have us believe otherwise. I'll have it ready for you in minutes. Then you can return to your sister, drink the medicine, and snap her out of it yourself. How does that sound?"

"Oh, that sounds wonderful!" As preposterous as this plan was, Esther dared to hope. "I can't thank you enough."

"Okay, no reason to fuss." She patted Esther's hand, removing it from her arm. "Now you must be quiet and let me concentrate."

She snatched bottles off the shelves and hung a cauldron over the fire. Esther watched her work with fascination. The woman poured one liquid after another into the cauldron, sniffing at the steam that rose from it, then, muttering to herself, she added another ingredient, and another. Soon a unique smell filled the cottage, but Esther found it not unpleasant.

"Valerian root has to steep first..." the widow explained, throwing two handfuls of what looked like twigs into the cauldron before bustling across the room to her shelf. "Owl's wing," she whispered, then winked at Esther. Holding up red foxglove, she sang, "Fingers of a birth-strangled babe, ditch delivered."

Esther smiled at the Shakespeare quote, surprised the widow didn't add, "Boil, boil, toil and trouble" as she continued to toss ingredients into the boiling cauldron. The smell turned quite unpleasant at last, and Esther wondered how much longer she could wait as the widow dropped a handful of dead moths into the mixture, saying, "Dream, dream, the dreaming, the teaming, the screaming, the gleaming, dream, dream..."

Esther gazed outside—the forest almost completely dark now.

"Ouch!" she cried. "Wha—"

"All part of the recipe, my dear," the widow chirped, throwing Esther's hair into the mixture with a flourish. "And...finished!"

She placed a small glass bottle in Esther's hands, the contents surprisingly cold.

"It only needs one more ingredient before you drink it."

"Yes?" Esther found herself impatient to return to Kitty, to try this plan out.

"Your sister's blood," the widow said, and Esther recoiled. "Now, now, don't look so horrified. Only a few drops should do. One drop for every hour you wish to remain joined with her thoughts. Two drops, two hours, three drops, three hours. But the spell will allow no more than three, you see. You will not be able to wake until the time is up, so choose wisely. And if any goblin should see you, there will be nothing you can do but try to survive."

Witchcraft. There could be no doubt. But would it work? Esther had to try, no matter the risks to her soul.

As if sensing Esther's determination, the witch smiled wide, and Esther's blood turned to ice. The same front tooth as Winifred's rotted in her foul mouth. Had the witch had been *disguised* as Esther's dear friend? Esther slowly backed away; the bottle held tightly in her grasp.

The witch followed her, smiling wider yet. "What's the matter, my dear? You look as if you've seen a ghost."

Had she?

"What have you done with my friend?" Esther whispered, though she dreaded to hear the answer.

"Did you know she lives in Bethnal Green?" The witch paused. "*Lived*, anyway. Old Nichol Street, to be precise. A particularly squalid corner of the most miserable slum in London. Did you know? She was starving, miserable, and lonely. You didn't care, did you? No, you didn't plan on ever visiting her, did you? Admit it, I won't blame you."

Esther couldn't speak; remorse and horror thrummed through her.

"The potion *will* work," the witch said. "I've been watching over you and your sister closely since your mother and aunt were murdered, knowing that the goblins weren't finished yet. This is the key to getting what I yearn for, and now you will barter with me."

Esther's lower lip wobbled. She itched to flee the witch's cottage, but she couldn't, not with her sister's life at risk. "Of course. Anything. What do you want?"

The witch rubbed her chin. "Regardless of whether you and your sister survive, I want the memories of your time there and you must bring me a piece of goblin fruit. Oh yes, and your sister's first-born child will be mine."

"No." Esther shook her head, suddenly filled with fear. Kitty would never agree to such a thing, though Esther desperately wanted to say yes. "Any future offspring will remain in my sister's belly. There must be another way."

At that, the witch transformed with rage, screaming as she flew at Esther. Esther barely dodged her grasp, spinning from her reach only to find her way to the door blocked. She inched away as the witch advanced, laughing at her fear. Her back against a shelf, Esther reached blindly behind herself, and threw the first thing her hand touched at the witch. The sound of shattering glass joined the woman's screams of rage. Bottle after bottle hit the witch as Esther continued to throw, never letting go of the potion she held, even as the woman lunged forward. A bottle almost too large for Esther to hold smashed against the stone floor at the widow's feet. The instant before it left her hand, the witch's eyes widened in fear and she raised her arms in protest, but it was too late. A deafening scream filled the cottage, and the witch disappeared in a cloud of foul-smelling smoke.

Esther stood panting against the counter in the silence as the air cleared. The fire crackled, candles burned brightly against the colorful knitted blankets, and a single toad blinked baleful, gold-tinted eyes up at her for a long second.

Then it exploded in a puddle of dark blood, the witch no more.

And Esther fled with the potion.

Seven

KITTY

itty twirled around the garden ballroom, dancing amongst the fiery poppies, snowy lilies, and saffron-hued daffodils that bloomed from the mossy floor and vine-covered walls beneath a glittering sky-blue ceiling. Silver dragonflies fluttered around her, their wings creating their own music, mirroring the lovely sounds of flutes.

It was the second evening of the kingdom's celebrations for their new queen. The night before in Errol's bed had been magical, like a dazzling dream, Kitty's happiness more complete than anything she could've imagined.

As she lifted a lily, inhaling its intoxicating scent, her gaze met the king's, and her heart leapt with joy. Errol watched her from his golden throne, branches curving around him in a mandala of oak, giving him a godlike appearance. His beauty radiated, and Kitty's breath caught at the sight of him. She couldn't get enough of this life, this heaven. The dancing, the eating, and the pleasuring: all hers, whenever she desired.

Kitty smiled at Errol, then let her gaze roam across the room. Dark clouds crossed over the sky-ceiling, and a nagging sensation of *wrongness* tugged at her mind.

"Esther," she murmured.

The crowd stilled as one, their gazes turning upon Kitty. "We love Esther," they said. "We want her with us as much as you."

Kitty halted. Her mother and aunt were nowhere to be found, which meant they hadn't returned with Esther. Perhaps everything was not so perfect after all. How could she have forgotten her sister wasn't here yet? Why couldn't she be here? Then everything would truly be complete.

Was Esther not at the bakery? Or their home? What if Esther never came?

Something wet pricked her eyes, and Kitty blinked, pressing her fingers to her cheeks, where they came away dewy. Tears. She was *crying*. But how could that be? This kingdom, this husband, it was all her dreams come true.

No, she mustn't ever cry. "Soon enough, Esther will join us here, and we will all be happy together," she vowed to herself, to everyone in the room.

Kitty cast a glance toward her king, knowing he could cure whatever ailed her, knowing he would grant her whatever she wanted, always. Grasping the silk of her skirts, she broke through the crowd and rushed to his side.

"Something is wrong with me," Kitty sobbed, holding out her hands as tears continued to pour down her cheeks.

"Come here, darling." Errol gathered her into his lap, his arms cradling Kitty while she cried into his chest. "Nothing could ever be wrong with you, my love."

Why wouldn't the tears stop? Why, even during her kingdom's celebrations, did it feel as if her heart would break?

Kitty closed her eyes and pictured Esther's face through the years: always her closest friend, always someone she wanted to follow.

"I need my sister," she pleaded. Straightening, her gaze met his. "I will search for her. I know Esther as well as I know myself. I can find her; I know I can."

Errol's gaze softened, and he wiped Kitty's lingering tears away. "My courageous queen, I will not stop you, if that is your heart's desire. Though it would break my own."

"I don't understand."

"Because, my sweet love, if you leave this world, you will never be able to return. We would never find each other again. Is that truly what you want?"

Horror washed over Kitty at the thought of separating from Errol for even a day. Yet forever? That was utterly unthinkable. To never touch him. To never taste his skin. To give up his intoxicating fruit, to not savor its sweetness again.

"No," she said. "Never."

Errol nodded, though the sadness in his eyes matched her own. Kitty knew he would do everything in his power to bring Esther to her.

"Remember, we have not received terrible news as of yet."

Something in his gaze made her still, a single treacherous thought bleeding inside her mind. Was he lying to her?

"For now," he continued, "I have something that I think will make you feel better." His eyes filled with mischief, and he held a finger toward her. Thick scarlet juice slid down its elegant length, enticing Kitty, and a ravenous hunger stirred within her as she studied the alluring liquid.

Esther. Esther. Esther.

Kitty couldn't deny what rested before her and leaned

closer toward the king, the smell of sweet fruit caressing her senses.

Esther...

She curled farther into the king's lap and clutched his wrist, moaning as she took his finger between her lips, her tongue swirling around the juice until she licked every bit clean.

"That's a good girl," Errol purred, trailing kisses across her jaw before slipping his tongue into her mouth to entwine with hers.

"More," she whispered, pouting as his lips left hers.

She opened her eyes and discovered the others had gone. They were alone. He tilted his head back, and Kitty brightened as she noticed Errol's tunic was no longer there. Crimson juice slid down his neck and bare chest, awaiting her tongue.

NIGHT AFTER NIGHT, THE CELEBRATIONS continued. But when Kitty opened her eyes this time, she no longer felt like dancing. Her appetite never satisfied, no matter how much fruit and wine she tasted. She roamed the halls, despondent, wishing for the sight of her king, as if in a stupor as the palace prepared for yet another night of festivities. At last, when the sun set along hills of lavender, her mother and aunt appeared after their long absence.

"Did you find Esther?" Kitty asked, rushing forward, her heart pounding while awaiting their answer. The crowd stilled to listen with her.

Her mother smiled wide. "She will join us soon, my sweet."

Kitty's shoulders fell. "I don't understand. Where is she?"

"Soon," Aunt Lizzie echoed Kitty's mother. "She is safe and well."

As Kitty opened her mouth to demand a proper answer, her mother held a pomegranate out to her, already opened, its insides shining like sparkling rubies. "For you."

Kitty could think of nothing but its sweetness while snatching the fruit from her mother, devouring it until at last joy filled her once more, as it always had, as was only right. She had always been perfectly happy.

Content.

Hadn't she?

A strong arm encircled her waist, a finger covered in red juice trailing her lips. Kitty leaned into her king's touch, relieved that he had finally arrived to join in the evening's celebrations.

"I missed you," she murmured.

"I was in misery without you, without you feeding my *hunger*," Errol whispered. "However, I have another surprise for you." He grinned, his love for her glowing within his sapphire eyes. The king clasped her hand, leading Kitty to a wall where a set of opening doors appeared. The crowd clapped as Kitty's lips parted, her heart leaping in elation at the sight before her.

The doors closed and they stood alone at last, together in the most gorgeous garden Kitty had ever set eyes on. Yew trunks of purple, blue, yellow, and pink stood majestically beneath bronze foliage, their leaves sparkling beneath a brilliant sky of pure gold.

Kitty whirled to face her king. "My own secret garden! You've given me a special gift each day." She frowned, her tears threatening to return. "And yet, I have nothing to offer you."

So many beloved things had been given to her. A silver stag, a library where books floated down to her when she called to them, and even a magical golden flute that taught her how to play. And now this masterpiece.

"You've given me all of you," Errol said, tucking a lock of hair behind her ear. "That is the only gift I desire. For you to remain in my world as my queen."

Kitty cradled his face and brought his lips to hers, kissing him until she grew dizzy with passion. She would please him the way she knew she could—she would make his smile glow brighter than it already did. They would make love as the golden sun set, and they would refuse to break apart until it rose again.

She reached for the laces of his trousers, then tugged the fabric down and knelt before her king.

KITTY DREW BACK THE SILKEN SHEETS AND LEFT the bed to prepare for the next celebration. Her gaze fell to the desk where a new platter of fruit awaited her. With a smile, she lifted a lush plum between her teeth. She moaned in delight as the juice drifted down her throat.

But her craving lingered still.

She glanced back at the bed, where Errol slept peacefully, his long lashes dusting his cheeks.

Taking a breath, she padded into the bathing chamber to find the tub already filled and ready for her. Steam wafted up from the water, beckoning her toward it. She slipped her nightgown from her shoulders and let the fabric pool at her feet.

Kitty stepped into the bath, the aroma of strawberries consuming her as the water's warmth cradled her. Bubbles formed around her, their sweet scent deliciously strong. She sighed in contentment, then lifted a cherry soap bar and scrubbed at her skin. A song left her lips—she'd never used to sing, not until she came to this wonderful world.

This magical kingdom had transformed her into a more joyous, more lively version of herself. As Kitty scrubbed, her movements became harder, rougher. It was as if her mind were peeling back its layers, and she could think of nothing but her sister, continuing day and night to slave away over a hot oven at the bakery. Alone. Missing Kitty in the way Kitty was missing her now.

It was the only thing absent from her perfect life, her perfect paradise—her sister left behind. Tears stung Kitty's eyes once again, and she didn't understand why her heart was suddenly breaking.

Her sister would be here soon—her mother and aunt had promised her this.

Errol's footsteps sounded, drawing closer, until he appeared in the doorway. His face softened with sympathy as his gaze met hers. He gently took the soap from Kitty's hands. "Is there anything I can do, my love? Why do you cry again? Are you not satisfied here? Do I not please you?"

"You do. Very much." But just the same, her lower lip wobbled, her hands shook. "Yet Esther...she is all alone."

"Soon," Errol vowed. "I will collect her myself if I must. I promise you that. Only, she will be more willing to come with your aunt and mother, don't you agree?"

Kitty frowned. "That's true. When Mother tells her I'm here, she'll come. I know she will."

"Certainly she will," Errol said, a smile spreading across his face. "I have a surprise that may cheer you up." He drew something from behind his back, something undeniably miraculous.

Kitty squealed. He held a bowl of pomegranate out for her, and she giddily plucked the fruit from his hand. These were her favorite; the fruit she could never get enough of. After consuming all of it, she still needed something more—her king.

"Before we celebrate," Kitty said, "I want you to do something for me." She blinked innocently, then her lips curled as she invited him into the bath with her. "You haven't been thoroughly washed yet, my king."

Errol smiled impishly. "A request that is easily granted, my love." He unfastened his trousers and let her slide them down his hips, his skin like perfect silk, his shape more exquisite than carved marble. He pulled her onto his lap as he entered the bath, the strawberry waters mixing with his irresistible scent. His lips found hers, and Kitty moaned, forgetting everything as the flavor of his sweet fruit enveloped her senses.

Their kisses deepened, desire coursing through her until suddenly the taste of decay filled her mouth, and she recoiled. She fell back into his arms as exhaustion rolled through her, her eyes fluttering closed, her body limp, her tongue heavy in her mouth.

Perhaps the devil was coming for her and her king, envious of their happiness.

"My love," Errol purred, setting a sweet raspberry against her tongue. "Are you well?"

Kitty opened her eyes while chewing the delicious fruit, not comprehending why she'd stopped kissing her king. "Of course," she breathed, then pressed her lips to his once more, relishing the ever present taste of him.

He kissed her in all the perfect places, showing how much he truly cared. And then Errol pleasured Kitty in the way only he knew, the only man who ever would.

As long as their lovemaking lasted, thoughts of her sister remained at bay.

Eight

ESTHER

"You can leave after I make certain the witch's potion works, Duncan," Esther said when she returned from the witch's cottage. "I won't fault you for it." A naïve part of herself had hoped to come home to find her sister blessed by some miracle: her skin blooming with youth, her nonsensical ramblings once again words Esther could understand. But there had been no miracle. Kitty lay there, her withered face staring blankly at the ceiling. Her heart steadily beat, though she looked dead.

"I won't leave you two alone and unconscious here." Duncan tipped a glass of water against Kitty's cracked lips and succeeded in forcing a little down Kitty's throat.

If she'd called on the physician again, she believed he would take Kitty away, study her withered body until she was nothing but a corpse. Perhaps continue his studies while she rotted and decayed in death.

"If Kitty awakens," Esther said, "promise me, you'll take her to a village dance, Duncan. I know that will make her smile."

Duncan blinked, his gaze holding hers before he focused on Kitty. "I'll dance with her until the sun rises, if it will make her smile."

Esther's eyes filled with tears, and she blinked them away. "You're a good man," she told him. "And an even better friend."

Lifting the edge of the blankets, Esther found Kitty's pale hand. She winced as she brought the needle to her sister's withered thumb and punctured the skin. Three drops of dark blood fell into the witch's bottle, changing the contents color from silver gray to a deep green.

"I'm sorry," Esther whispered, kissing Kitty's hand. "Wait for me, sister. Please. I will search for you, and I will make this right, do you understand? We must both be brave now."

The silence was deafening as Kitty only stared at the ceiling, leaving Esther alone with her living corpse.

After collecting a Döbereiner's lamp, the tiny ether bottle the doctor had prescribed to Kitty, and an iron poker from the fireplace for her best line of defense, Esther lay on the bed next to Kitty's still form and prepared herself to take the witch's potion. The stench of mildew and rotting flesh mixed with cinnamon and treacle permeated the air. Esther nearly gagged as she put the bottle to her lips, but she closed her eyes and ignored her revulsion.

The witch hadn't said how much she should drink.

Suddenly the bottle appeared enormous to her, and Esther took a deep breath, searching for the courage to drink its foul-smelling contents. What if she failed? The witch was dead and could make no more magic, impersonate no more unsuspecting pawns, murder no more innocent souls. Like her poor dear friend Winifred...

There weren't tomes that told of what to expect upon

entering the goblin world, no other villagers had survived venturing into it. All Esther knew of the other victims came from the stories her mother and aunt had told her. The fruit made one see false beauty, as her mother had. While Aunt Lizzie had tricked a goblin to take her to the world without eating the fruit and had seen hideous things of nightmares.

Esther considered adding yet another few drops of blood to the liquid, wondering if it could multiply her time in Kitty's mind, but studying the swirling green liquid before her, she worried she had lost the chance to alter the potion further and dared not risk destroying it. If the witch had lied about everything, and this concoction actually killed her, it was still worth the risk to try and save her sister.

Raising the bottle, Esther gathered her nerve and toasted over the forlorn scene, "To Kitty's good health and steadfast courage. May each day bring more happiness than the day before it." *Please.*

Esther drank.

She drank even as the potion burned like hot coals tumbling down her throat, and she continued until the very last drop. Until the world around her turned to darkness.

ESTHER AWOKE TO FIND SHE LAY AGAINST WARM grass softer than any bed she had ever known, the iron poker still clutched in her grasp. Golden light bathed trees in shades of deep emerald above her—blooms of every color and size spread out around her. One rose leaned over her, as if to kiss her cheek.

Disoriented, Esther sat, and for one terrible instant the

world grew cold and pitch-black before slipping back into paradise.

The potion had *worked*. Esther could feel, smell, and hear everything as if her surroundings were real. She pinched herself, surprised by the pain.

"Hello?" she called out. "Kitty? Are you here?"

The only answer she received was birdsong.

"I am within the goblin world and seeing it as Kitty would," Esther told herself, closing her eyes and breathing deeply.

She rose to her feet and turned in a slow circle, surveying her surroundings. A small herd of deer leapt over a sparkling brook, their dappled fur shimmering in the sun's warm glow. From a branch, a bird the color of Spanish bluebells watched her, tilting its head inquisitively before taking flight. And there, far in the distance, a storm brewed, dark and ominous.

"Right, then," Esther said, ignoring the dread filling her heart, and marched forward as lightning streaked across the sky's blood-red surface. "That must be the way."

With each step she took, Kitty's paradise around her faded, replaced by Esther's own sight since she'd not tasted the goblin fruit. She stilled, her chest heaving, her heart pounding fiercely. It was as if the comfort of a summer garden was nothing but a ghostly illusion. A photograph placed over Esther's eyes, double exposing her reality.

The goblins' world was a cold and terrifying place, its desolation matching that of the creatures' evil wickedness. She couldn't help but think of her mother and aunt, how they'd once defeated these vicious creatures. But even that victory had been short-lived. The goblins had come for her family in the end. Esther promised herself that if she and her sister got out of this, the goblins would never find them again.

Branches reached out like clawed fingers, oozing sap akin to blood against their charred, jagged surface. She stuck to the path, though she trembled discovering the trail littered with broken bones.

The monstrous trees grew ever thicker, limbs bowing across the path like a cage. Esther hunched into the cold, continuing forward with renewed determination even as screams from within the dark forest filled the foul, sulphury air.

The bones along the path seemed to come to life as something large approached, shaking the world. Esther halted. There was nowhere to seek cover, except within the terrible tendril-like trees. She hesitated, her heart thundering faster until she was sure it would burst.

"You must not be seen," she whispered. "Find Kitty and wake her from this nightmare, whatever it takes."

Esther dove into the trees just as a carriage came into view. Pulled by three canine-like beasts the size of ponies—hellhounds—their sight more dreadful than anything she could've imagined. The creatures' moldy fur fell away in mangy clumps, their ribs exposed in horrible relief, and their glowing eyes looked crazed. They skidded to a stop, sniffing the air, their rotting fangs protruding from boil-infested gums. One pitiful iron poker would do nothing against the lot of them.

Esther held her breath as the beasts grew ever closer. Their noses appeared like open septic wounds, their breath, revolting even from feet away. For an instant, she could see once again through Kitty's eyes—paradise enveloped the scene, revealing the hounds as nothing but three harmless pine martens. The adorable creatures cheerfully sniffed at berries in the golden sunlight. A field of daisies and thistle swayed lazily beneath pollen dust motes as bees drank nectar from honeysuckle.

Esther knew better than to move. The menacing hell-hounds were the reality. The pain of their bite would be all too true if she were found.

As the lead hound's nose nearly touched Esther's skin, the creature suddenly screamed in pain, flinching with a violence that almost made Esther fall. For the first time, the coach's terrible driver was revealed to her as his whip slashed across the hellhound's already destroyed fur with a string of vile curses.

Based on her aunt's horrid descriptions of a true goblin's face, it had to be one.

Beneath a ghostly exterior of a man of surpassing beauty, golden skin and exotic feathers decorating enviable hair, the creature's true form showed through as the carriage passed. The world had never known a face which held more cruelty than that of the goblin. Eyes as ice-cold as a bitter winter night, it grimaced to reveal rows of needle-like teeth. Dull green scales covered its skin. Its knobby hands ended with sharp claws, seizing the carriage reins.

Esther shuddered, picturing poor Kitty surrounded by such horrific creatures, and clutched the poker. But as she stepped forward, Esther realized with a jolt of nausea that she couldn't move. Vines, like clenched fingers, gripped her ankles and climbed her calves.

She swiped at them with her poker, but the vines didn't let up.

"We sssssee you, pretty poppet," something whispered

from the shadows. Esther clamped a hand over her mouth to stop her scream.

The trees around her moved, their veiny branches reaching for her face, and Esther swatted at them frantically, struggling to free her legs in vain. Lightning struck again, illuminating her nightmare, and finally Esther screamed. Instead of leaves or flowers, the tree branches were covered in dozens of eyes, all of them trained on her.

I'm so sorry I failed you, Kitty, Esther thought as she fell. The branches engulfed her in their cold embrace, the poker tumbling from her grasp. *May God forgive my cowardice.*

And then the Döbereiner's lamp jostled in her pocket, reminding her that she hadn't truly failed yet.

Esther opened her eyes, forcing herself to remain still as she considered her position. It seemed her fate wasn't to be killed, but rather *moved*—she trembled, wondering where. Esther didn't care to be taken charge of by any devilish creature.

So you must think!

The trees appeared to all be connected, working together in synchronicity against their human invader, as if of one single mind. If she could injure one, perhaps she might injure them all.

Esther had to hope—it was all she had left. Without hope, she might as well die now, leaving her sister to starve.

Moving ever so slowly as she was passed from one branch to the next, Esther reached into her cloak for the Döbereiner's lamp. The cylindrical tinder box fit nicely in her hand, and Esther held it still within her pocket, cloaked by darkness as hundreds of unblinking eyes remained fixed on her. She would have one chance to fight. Holding the lighter in one hand, she searched her left pocket for the tiny bottle of ether. Praying the flammable liquid would be enough, Esther acted.

Pressing down on the tinder box's valve, her heart leapt as the pressure built within its inner chamber to light the hydrogen flame. Fire came to life with a soft *click* and a warm glow. No time to waste, she poured the ether onto the closest vine's eye socket, holding the blazing lighter to the liquid. Esther shouted in triumph as she watched it explode into flame.

A high-pitched shriek left her ears ringing, and all at once the vines released her. The flames grew to a mighty inferno, as if the blood in their veinlike branches were gin.

She hit the ground with a bone-jarring *thump*, tasting blood when her teeth cut into her tongue. Esther ignored the pain and scrambled to her feet. She collected the iron poker, realized the lighter had been lost in the chaos, and ran.

With no idea where the bone-strewn path was—and not sure she'd want to follow it even if she did unearth it again—Esther continued toward the storm's center in the distance. Lightning guided her through the darkness as the trees burned to ashes. The wretched screams of the forest dying down while the stench of rot and sepsis steadily worsened.

Over a hill and through a valley of jagged rock, a light rain, that stung her skin, fell from the sky. A new variety of forest stood before her. Esther refused to look too closely at the vegetation as she passed by, the rounded stems reminding her of severed heads. She stuck to wide meadows of blackish mud, trying not to think of quicksand, while blinking away the illusion of a crimson and yellow poppy-field paradise that threatened to overtake her senses.

How many minutes had it been now?

"Do not give up hope, Kitty," she whispered. "We are not defeated yet."

The trees grew sparser, until they disappeared altogether, along with any semblance of a path. Esther found herself in a vast desert as she followed the gathering storm. She quickened her pace until she was running again for what felt like ages, terrified her three hours would come to an end before she found Kitty.

At last Esther halted, her heart thundering not from exertion, but horror.

Beyond the wide expanse of desolate, black desert stood a castle. Dark as a moonless night, its many towers stood against the storm-filled sky, akin to a vicious set of fangs.

And Esther knew, beyond any doubt, Kitty was within those walls.

Nine

KITTY

"Mother, Mother," Kitty pleaded, pulling at her mother's skirts. "Tell me more about the goblins." Esther was already fast asleep, but no matter how long she lay in bed with her eyes closed, Kitty's thoughts continued to spin in her head, her wild imagination dragging her from her bed and back to her mother's side.

"You know you're supposed to be asleep, my sweet," her mother said, trying to look stern even as she lifted Kitty into her arms and rocked her back and forth. Kitty snuggled close, the creaking of the rocking chair a familiar comfort. "But all right. The goblins are creatures of darkness and trickery. They spew beautiful lies so as to make their victims feel brighter than the stars. Only to turn them into dust, buried deep in the dirt, cold and dark, cast away from everything and everyone they ever loved. Goblins make one forget who they are, what they are."

Kitty shivered, relishing the danger and adventure of such magical and impossible things. She straightened in her moth-

er's lap, determined to be the strong girl her family needed. "I would never allow them to do that to me," she said matter of fact. "Never ever ever!"

"Sometimes, no matter how brave we are, magic gets the better of us. Failure cannot always be helped. Sometimes, in fact, it is failure that is our best teacher." She tilted Kitty's face toward her and placed a kiss on her forehead. "Now we must get you back into bed, little one, or Esther will be cross in the morning when she finds you're unable to help take care of the chickens."

Her mother carried Kitty to bed, bringing the quilt up to her chin, and rested her stuffed kitten close beside her. "As you grow older, you won't ask about these stories any longer. But always remember that there are two types of kindness. True kindness, which is its own glorious reward and asks for nothing in return, and false kindness, which takes and takes until there is nothing left to take at all."

GOBLINS...THAT WORD...A WORD ALMOST forgotten.

Something squishy rested against Kitty's cheek and her eyes flew open. A thick, sticky substance cocooned her body, and she froze, horrified.

Goblins...

The scent of rot invaded her senses, a *familiar* smell. When she was...when she was...

She couldn't quite grasp the memory.

A buzzing pulsed just above her ear. Kitty trembled, her heart hammering as she twisted around in the enveloping liquid to find tiny skeletal monsters with leathery wings. They flew around her in the dim light, hissing, their sharp fangs protruding from their grimacing, horrible faces. Their round, milky-white eyes stared.

Kitty opened her mouth to scream, but no sound escaped her. Too afraid to even push herself up, she gasped, gagging against the stench of rotten eggs. She remembered falling asleep outside the night before, yet here she lay, no longer in her beautiful garden of dreams and golden light. Instead, the world had turned a murky gray, her garden nothing but oozing decay and rot. Grotesque beasts, half her size, hobbled around the wilted skeletons of trees, watching her with hungry, glowing eyes. Their skin was the red and black of burnt flesh, and boils covered their grotesque faces.

Cackles pierced Kitty's skull, reverberating across the gloom, louder and louder until it felt as if the sound would burst her eardrums. As madness consumed her, at last she found the strength to sit. With a gasp of horror, she discovered that the sticky substance surrounding her wasn't mud but *blood*. Puddles of crimson surrounded her, more pooling around the bases of the dead trees. Kitty scrambled backward with a cry, shoving to her feet.

Deep down, she knew what this was, in the way she knew her very heart. Kitty closed her eyes, refusing to scream in terror. She took slow breaths as the vile creatures watched her with beady gazes, their toothy grins taunting her.

"Remember, Kitty," she pleaded, pulling at her hair, slapping her cheeks, trying to recall what she'd been warned about. She had not a single weapon to protect herself. She was trapped and terrified, a cornered animal.

An arm draped around her waist then, and Kitty flinched. But before she could turn, a finger covered in juice brushed her lips, tasting of pure heaven. An instant calm washed over Kitty. Her body relaxed—her fear dissipated. No longer was she in a pit of despair surrounded by the beasts of nightmares, but she was once again in her comforting garden. Sprites danced above her. Deer and rabbits gracefully leapt through the trees of purple, blue, yellow, and pink.

Had she been dreaming?

"Only a nightmare, my love," Errol's alluring voice whispered in her ear, soft lips against her neck as he slowly breathed her in, her muscles wilting for a fraction of a moment. She grew tired... Exhausted...

Gently, he turned her in his arms to face him, his shining blue eyes strengthening her. He kissed her lightly, his flavor like the sweetest nectar. "I'm here. I'll always protect you."

Kitty opened her mouth to tell him about her nightmare, what she'd seen, how her insides felt like a drooping flower, when he brought a peach to her lips. One look at its velvety blush-rich skin and she couldn't stop herself from sinking her teeth into it. The juice's sweetness soared through her, and she felt as though she were flying. Her nightmare faded, the ghastly images slipping farther away, replaced instead with bliss.

"It wasn't a nightmare, after all. It was a beautiful dream." Kitty smiled, gazing into Errol's sapphire eyes. A perfect dream that was just as perfect as this kingdom and her otherworldly husband.

After she finished her peach, Errol cooed, his breath hot on her neck, "I brought you some of these from my special garden as well. This is the only time of year they grow." He lifted a golden bowl of dazzling red cherries, and Kitty's heart leapt in delight. She hungrily ate the fruit, pleasurable sighs escaping her. As she swallowed the last of them, Kitty realized she hadn't left him a single one.

"I'm sorry. I'm a greedy little thing this morning." She laughed, licking the remaining juice from her lips.

"We have an abundance here. Always eat as much as you desire," he purred, twirling a lock of her golden hair around his finger. "I have another gift for you, my queen. Shall I take you to see it?"

Kitty perked up at once. "Oh yes!" she cried. Errol was such a gracious king and husband—so giving, so thoughtful.

The king helped her to her feet and gently kissed her lips. "Go to the library, and I'll meet you there shortly."

Kitty's heart swelled as she hurried to the library, her pulse racing with anticipation. The day before, Errol had painted a portrait of Esther for her.

"Her hair is the richest of golds, her eyes light blue. Esther's nose is smaller than mine, her cheekbones high." Kitty tilted her head, describing her sister's features the best she could as Errol painted, his brush gliding across the canvas.

"How does it look?" he asked, and as Kitty leaned over him to see, he nuzzled his face into her neck, making her smile.

But her smile slipped as she studied his artwork. Every detail matched Esther precisely, even the small scar beside Esther's eye where she'd fallen as a child against the corner of the supper table.

"It's perfect," she murmured, squeezing his hand gently. "Thank you, my king."

The palace was empty of guests, the sweet scent of berries clinging to the morning air. Kitty ascended the glass staircase and ventured down the hallway to the library door, already drawn open for her. She stared up at the portrait of her sister, and an instant calm filled her. But as she walked toward the center of the room where a chaise of green velvet sat, the eyes of her sister seemed to follow her. A chill crawled up Kitty's spine, and she shrugged off her foolishness. "You just want Esther here is all."

Kitty hadn't spent much time in the library yet, and walls of shelves, reaching as tall as the ceiling, surrounded her. A violet fire crackled in one corner, a fur rug of some exotic beast before it.

Clasping her hands in front of her, Kitty pored over a row of books until she found a fairytale she'd never heard of. "I choose you." In answer, the tome slipped from the book-shelf and flew into her grasp. She lowered herself onto the chaise, sinking deep into the cushions, making her feel as if she were floating on a cloud.

Before she could fully immerse herself in the princess's story, Errol's boots echoed through the hallway.

Kitty snapped the book closed and leapt to her feet as he sauntered toward her, something tiny and blue in his arms. A *kitten*. It lifted its head, meowing, meek and pitiful, and her heart melted.

Errol held the kitten up, his face hesitant. "I hope you like her. I want you to have a friend when you need one and I'm not around."

"Oh my goodness! I love her!" She giggled, reaching eagerly for the creature. "A kitten with fur that matches your eyes!" As she held the adorable little creature, she laughed in delight, its fur as soft as the silk sheets of Errol's bed.

With each stroke of her hand, the kitten's fur changed color in the candlelight, at once indigo, then cobalt, teal, and periwinkle. So many shades of blue. It purred, blinking wide gold-flecked eyes up at her.

"Nova." Kitty beamed. "I'm going to call her Nova."

"Nova is perfect." Errol smiled. "Look, she loves you already. Shall we have a seat in front of the fire?"

"Yes, please." She followed him to the fireplace and sat beside him on the fur rug. The flames warmed her flesh as she held the kitten tenderly.

Kitty placed Nova on the rug, and the kitten rolled to her back. She gently rubbed Nova's stomach and laughed while the creature continued to purr.

"I always wanted a kitten." Kitty sighed, locking her gaze on Errol's brilliant irises. "But we never had enough money to feed another mouth after my father and uncle died during the war. Besides the chickens, I used to pretend the animals outside our home were our pets. The insects, the birds, even the worms in the garden. And Esther, she would bring toads for me to play with before we carried them back to their pond. She's the loveliest sister. That day, when I went to the market, she told me I could get anything I wanted. She worried I was—"

"You're thinking a lot about your old world today," Errol interrupted, and Kitty could've sworn a line furrowed his brow, his eyes flashing with anger. But when she looked again, the expression was gone, replaced by his usual doting love and devotion. It had been her imagination, surely.

"I think...I miss more than just Esther," she murmured, taking Nova into her lap. Errol would understand how she felt—he always did. "I think I miss my village. My familiar, cold and rainy village, with its bustling shops and markets, the sound of the train's engine coming and going, and even the picky customers and cranky old women."

"I know just what will cure your melancholy." The king reached behind him, and Kitty craned her neck to see what fresh magic he held to brighten her mood. In his hands was a bowl of pomegranate. "This one is no ordinary fruit," he said, smiling wide. "It's extra special."

Kitty bit her lip, the delightful smell clouding her senses, her tongue begging for a taste of the wondrous juice. But even then, she didn't reach for a seed—she held back, some almost forgotten lesson tugging at her thoughts.

Shadows from the candles glided across the floor. What story had her mother told her as a child? What had she warned Kitty about? And as if lightning struck, the memory was there, and Kitty inhaled sharply, fear flooding through her.

Goblin men.

"I'm not hungry," Kitty whispered.

"You're always hungry, my love," Errol murmured, and even as she leaned away from him, he pushed the fruit between her lips. There wasn't enough time to spit it out or even to war with herself because she *adored* the flavor too much. Adored the way the fruit took hold of her, adored the way the world brightened around her once more, the way only lovely images danced inside her mind. It was the most delicious fruit she'd had, more delicious than the rest.

Kitty rushed to finish it all, and when the bowl sat empty, she only wished there were more. "What's so special about this one?" She had to know. "It is positively divine."

"It is a fruit given when necessary. For a truly special occasion. You're a rather strong one," he drawled. "Now, we must go downstairs, my queen. The celebrations are not over yet."

Kitty peered down at herself, gasping to see she no longer wore the gown he'd pleasured her in the night before—had it been blood-stained and ruined? *No, what a silly thought! No.* This gown was made of purple and red silk, silver and copper vines embellishing its bodice. Rubies and amethyst dripped from the hem. Her skirts swished as she stood.

Errol lifted her before she could walk, cradling her in his arms. "How about I take you downstairs like this and show the guests that I'm the one at your will."

Kitty giggled, kissing his cheeks, his nose, his mouth. "And then you can carry me upstairs afterward, straight into your bed."

His eyes grew hooded, his hands sensually gliding down her hips as he set her on her feet. "We may have to leave rather early if you continue to talk like that. Tonight I will taste you deeper, down to your very *soul*," he said, his smile wickedly beautiful. His gaze spoke of secrets, but her king didn't keep any secrets from her, did he? *Of course not*!

Nova followed them downstairs in happy leaps, purring all the while, and they entered yet another ballroom. A magical crystal harp played delicate music, though no one plucked its strings. A crowd had already gathered, larger than any of the previous days. For this celebration, the guests wore glittering golden masks that covered their features entirely, even their eyes. It was a miraculous sight, as if they were all preparing for a jester to enter to use them like chess pieces in his act.

Errol bent toward Kitty's ear and said in a gruff voice, "I will be right back, my precious. There is something I need to take care of." He kissed Kitty deeply, letting her take in his intoxicating scent.

"Of course." Kitty nodded with a smile. Her eyes lingered on him as he vanished down the hallway.

She listened to instruments play a full three songs, then watched Nova weave through the crowd, directly to two women, the only ones not adorning masks. She recognized her mother and aunt at the crowd's center, their wild golden curls falling to their waists. When her mother's gaze met hers, she rushed toward Kitty, a smile in her voice behind her mask. "Your sister has arrived, my sweet."

Over the music, Kitty listened, and she could've sworn she heard Esther's voice—distant, shouting something just beyond her understanding.

Ten

ESTHER

A warm breeze ruffled Esther's hair as the roaring bellow of alligators filled the goblin-world night, and she trembled in fear.

Her throat grew parched, begging for a drink of the devilish things this place had to offer. She closed her eyes, thinking of Kitty, remembering happier times. Visiting Barron's mansion to tour his private menagerie felt so long ago, and she could still feel Kitty's hand clutching hers while they took in the sight of animals they'd never seen before.

She knew the monsters in the darkness to be more frightening than any alligator.

Esther slid another foot forward, her throat burning. Squinting, she found a door embedded in the rocks.

"I'm coming, Kitty," she said with renewed determination. "I'm coming."

The castle loomed closer with each step, the spires atop its ebony turrets growing like the claws of a giant cat. Though she trembled, Esther continued forward until its jagged outer fortifications blocked out the blood-red sky. Her mother had been fortunate enough to have never encountered the Goblin King, but if Aunt Lizzie hadn't rescued her all those years ago, Esther was certain he would have been her mother's fate.

The place appeared to have only one entrance. Esther stared in dismay at the castle's spikey portcullis, its towering iron grid blocking a narrow and treacherously rotted bridge that led across a dark abyss of a moat. Esther imagined she could see the stars of endless galaxies within the depths of the moat, and a wave of vertigo washed over her.

"Right," she muttered, steadying herself against a boulder. "There's no way that entrance is not guarded."

As the last words left her lips, mist rose from the ground, taking the shape of ghostly soldiers, solid within moments. Moss covered their rusted armor. Insects and snakes moved along the figures, who marched forward as one, forming a semicircle around the castle's entrance, blades drawn. The sky blazed every color of flame. Esther gasped at the hollow-eyed soldiers' skeletal faces, their skin rotting away from pale bone.

She stumbled back into the cover of darkness, stifling a scream.

How much time did she have left?

Esther retreated silently, though her feet were like ice and her heart thundered. She was determined to find another entrance to the castle, and prayed, *willing* Kitty to help guide her way. For Esther knew with absolute certainty that her sister's consciousness, her mind, perhaps her very soul—no matter how impossible it seemed—was being kept inside. She had faith that some part of Kitty, if only a sliver, had been guiding her thus far.

Esther had walked only a few minutes before she regretted her decision.

"I should've tried my luck with the living dead soldiers," she breathed. "Oh, Kitty..."

The sight turned Esther's stomach. Creatures who appeared to be put together from slaughtered animals and humans alike tended an orchard by the warm light of a hundred lanterns. Their backs were hunched, their macabre faces fixed in concentration. It was true that the fruit hanging from the rows of branches was beautiful beyond belief, but as Esther watched, she discovered what soil fed the fruit. What water poured from the castle to flow along the orchard rows.

The pitiful remains of young women dropped from the castle's worn battlement, their naked limbs frail and thin as they floated like falling angels, and landing as crumpled and twisted as marionettes with their strings cut atop a growing mountain of the dead.

Trapped souls.

Was this Kitty's fate? Were these the bodies of those who'd been tricked or foolish enough to have tasted the goblins' forbidden fruit?

As Esther stood frozen in horror, beetle-like creatures with nine legs and dull human faces gracing both the front and back of their bulbous heads shuffled forward. They gathered barrelful after barrelful of the remains, then dumped them like so much rubbish into a worn and weathered gristmill, where they were ground into a fine powder.

Esther's stomach churned as she watched, paralyzed with disgust and fear. More creatures—goblins resembling feathered hogs sporting twisted horns stood on two legs, like men

—collected the flour and distributed it amongst the lines of trees, watering the scorched earth with a deep red liquid.

"Dearest sister," she whispered. "I pray to God this is not what you see."

As if in answer to her prayer, Esther's grisly vision overlapped with a perfect paradise. The castle, now made of crystal, quartz, ivory, and gold, stood beyond the orchard. The falling bodies transformed into a sparkling waterfall. A pool of perfect aquamarine reflected golden sunlight at its base. A garden of colorful roses graced its banks, birds swarming the foliage, and a magnificent, winged, white horse wandered along the grass, a velvet carpet of jade.

The trees of the orchard remained unchanged.

The tantalizing fruit caused Esther's hunger to stir— ravenous hunger she'd never felt before. She longed to taste the enormous plums nearest to her, but she controlled herself, willing her feet to remain rooted to the spot. Her hands longed to reach out to the fruit, and she forced her eyes to see what was *real*.

The scene of gore and dread fell into place once again, and Esther shook her head, nearly bursting into tears of frustration as she struggled to think of a way inside to get to Kitty.

"There you are," a voice like stone purred into her ear. Esther gasped as an icy hand gripped her arm with otherworldly strength, leaving her no room to wield the iron poker at him.

"Majesty, I've found the rodent problem!"

"I saw her first!" another voice protested.

"We all saw her. She's standing in full sight," a third whined. "We should all get the reward."

"Do you think the reward will be her spleen?" the first groaned hungrily. "I love a good spleen!"

Esther turned to look at her captors, but just then a creature moved from the shadows who arrested her full attention, and her knees buckled with fear.

Towering above the orchard, the goblin could not be mistaken for any but this land's king. Both royal and terrifying, the creature strode forward into the lamplight. His skin appeared to be made of moving vines, every shade of living green and dying, bloodied rot. His red eyes matched the sky, pupils a swirl of stars complimenting the abyss surrounding his castle. Not an ounce of beauty could be found among his crown—golden fruit decorated intricately carved charred bones. As he closed the gap between them, death wafted off him, decayed plants and flesh alike, and she nearly gagged.

"No cheating," he seethed, his voice like distant thunder. It took all of Esther's will not to flinch from him as he grazed his fingertips down her cheek, his touch like ice and fire. "You should know, dear Esther, mortals who have not yet tasted our fruit are not welcome here."

"A witch's concoction." The whining captor poked Esther's shoulder roughly.

"It's like"—the other poked at her back—"she's here, but not here at the same time."

Esther thrust her iron weapon at the Goblin King, and he ripped the poker from her hand. Hissing, he dropped it to the ground, where it vanished. Her heart lodged in her throat, but she set the defeat aside.

"I want to see my sister," Esther demanded, hoping her voice sounded stronger than she felt.

In response, the Goblin King leaned closer to her,

sniffing at her neck and face. His forked tongue darted over his vile lips, and this time Esther did shrink from him.

The Goblin King smirked. "Making demands, are we?"

"Will you allow me to trade anything for her? My life?"

"No." His eyes blazed with pleasure at the knowledge she'd be willing to forsake herself, and oh, how Esther loathed him for it. She wished for nothing but to end him. "And you think breaking into my home like a rodent will save her? Do you know what we do to sneaking, thieving criminals here?"

"Please..." Esther refused to cry in front of this monster even though she was on the brink of tears. "Let me see my sister. Let me speak to her, just once, and I promise I'll..."

The king's tongue flicked across his lips again, his teeth like filthy shards of broken glass. "You'll what?"

"I'll..." What did Esther have to offer him? She'd just offered her life which was already at his mercy—he'd destroyed everything she loved.

The Goblin King threw his vile head back and laughed, the others joining in. The sound made her feel as if insects and worms crawled up her flesh, and Esther shuddered.

Abruptly, his laughter ceased, and the Goblin King clapped his clawed hands together, grinning wickedly.

"I'll let you see Kitty, if you're certain that's what you want," he cooed. "I'll even allow you to speak to her."

Esther choked back a sob and would have fallen to her knees with relief had her captors not held her up.

"Tha—"

"Don't thank me, rodent." The Goblin King's eyes shone red, and he smiled wickedly. "I permit it for my own amusement. You see, there is nothing you can do or say to save her now. Kitty is mine, and your time will come soon enough."

Eleven

KITTY

"Kitty! Are you there?" a woman's voice echoed in the distance—desperate, searching.

Kitty knew that voice, clear as day. It was certainly Esther. Not Kitty's imagination. And her sister was calling to her. Searching for *her*.

Biting her lip, Kitty stared at her mother and aunt. Before she could utter a word, they both clasped their hands in encouragement and purred in unison, "Go to her. Bring your sister here safely."

Kitty lifted her silk skirts and broke through the crowd, their expressions still hidden behind their masks while they whispered and turned in her direction as she passed. This was what Kitty had been waiting for. For her loving sister to escape their pitiful world of cold and discomfort and enter this luxurious heaven. For Esther to come home. Where she would always be protected, always be happy.

A guard wearing golden armor and a helmet decorated with a white ostrich feather pulled open the palace door moments before she reached it. Kitty rushed outside, finding the air deliciously warm against her skin. She gasped in awe as a miniature Pegasus flew above her, followed by a group of equally fantastical creatures, their colors dazzling in the sunlight. They guided her in the direction of her sister's call while Kitty laughed and raced toward it.

Again, her name floated on the breeze, wild and frenzied.

"Kitty! Kitty, are you there?"

The voice held fear. How could anyone fear anything in such a land?

"Esther!" Kitty shouted, lifting her skirts higher so she could run yet faster and faster still. Her heart pounded, and her own fear grew. What if she never found her sister?

No, Errol had promised her.

Kitty's crystal heels clacked against the bridge as she raced across its golden planks. She was surprised they didn't break, but why would they? Her world was absolute perfection. Surrounded by magic, she could not make a single misstep.

As she reached the end of the bridge, Kitty scanned the forest, straining to decipher precisely where her sister's voice came from. She rushed forward to enter the woods, but Kitty's gaze latched on to something in the distance, emerging from the orchard of flowering apple trees. Three guards dressed in shimmering gold uniforms led between them a woman with a blonde braid wearing a familiar tattered dress.

Kitty almost collapsed in relief when her gaze met her sister's, and she shouted, "Esther! You're finally here!"

Worry didn't leave Esther's expression as she hurried forward to collide with her sister.

"Kitty!" Esther wrapped her arms around Kitty, the embrace warm and comforting, and held her close, squeezing her tightly, *too* tightly. "I found you," she whispered, and

Kitty wondered if Esther hoped the guards wouldn't hear her. "I will always come for you, sister. I haven't stopped searching since the day you...went missing. I'm sorry... I'm sorry it took me so long."

Esther released Kitty and stood back, her eyes darting between the guards as if she didn't trust them. Tears streamed down her face, and confusion swam through Kitty. Why wasn't Esther happy at this moment?

"But I've eaten the magical fruit," she continued brightly, her voice louder now that even the guards could hear. "And here I am. Isn't it wonderful?"

Kitty wiped the tears from Esther's cheeks. "There is nothing to fear here," she promised. "Nothing at all. You've left that awful place, and now we will never be apart. Let me take you inside the palace. There are so many magnificent and delightful surprises awaiting you!" She clasped her sister's wrist and tugged her across the bridge. The guards remained silent and close, their boots thudding in time with the sisters' steps as they followed them toward the awaiting palace doors.

"Kitty," Esther whispered again. "Can we perhaps find some lovely place to chat alone together? There is so much I wish to discuss in confidence with you." She smiled, but by the slightly turned-down edges of her lips, Kitty knew that for whatever reason the expression was forced. It was inconceivable. Esther only needed to see more of this wonderful utopia and then her sister would feel more relaxed, Kitty was sure of it.

"Soon. There are two people you need to see first!"

"All right. Then afterwards?"

"Of course, of course!" Kitty grasped Esther's hand and led her inside the palace, her sister unusually silent beside her.

Esther trembled slightly as they approached the waiting crowd within the ballroom, her gaze drifting across the sea of masked faces, then her false smile returned.

Kitty squeezed her sister's hand. "Esther, I vow on my life, you'll be happier here than you have ever been before. No more slaving away over a hot stove for ungrateful customers at the bakery, no more worrying if you'll wed someone who doesn't treat you with everlasting love and kindness, as you deserve. It's us together. Doing only what we choose."

The crowd spread apart, revealing the two women Kitty was searching for. "Look, sister! It's Mother and Aunt Lizzie! We haven't lost them after all."

Esther sucked in a sharp breath, and Kitty knew at once her sister was taken aback, at a loss for words, but nonetheless, pleased.

The two women walked toward them, their skirts swishing gracefully, as if they walked on air. Their movements were lithe, and their shining faces—beautiful.

"Esther, we searched and searched for you!" her mother said with a choked sob, gathering her daughter in her embrace.

"Look at us. All together again. Forever and ever. I've missed you so much." Aunt Lizzie draped her arms around her niece.

"I-I've missed you both," Esther stuttered, hugging them. "This place is lovely. *Magical*."

Something still wasn't right. The way Esther had said magical was as if she were nauseous and about to expel the contents of her stomach.

Esther was lying.

Her sister had always been the unrelentingly honest one,

while Kitty had told fibs every now and then, especially to avoid trouble. Was Esther not happy to see them? Did she prefer to be back in the mundane world without Kitty, where her mother and aunt were dead? Perhaps she was in love with someone there and wanted to go back to him? There had been a boy at a market... What was his name?

Regardless, no, that couldn't be it.

Esther's gaze dropped to Kitty's tattooed finger, and her eyes widened in surprise. "What is this, a golden stigmata?" She seemed to notice Kitty's crown for the first time and reached for it, hesitating. "And this?"

Kitty bit her lip, unable to hold back the delightful elation storming through her veins. She flashed her hand in front of her sister's face. "Oh, Esther, I'm married! The king chose me to be his queen; can you believe it? There is no doubt I've fallen completely, blissfully in love."

Esther choked, pressing a fist to her mouth as a rack of coughs escaped her, and she whispered, "*Married*? Husband? No. No, no, no, no."

"What's the matter, darling?" their mother asked. "Aren't you happy for your sister?"

"Yes, aren't you happy?" Aunt Lizzie added.

"I am," Esther sobered, that same fake smile curling her lips again. "I was just taken aback is all. I would've loved to have been at the wedding—I've truly missed so much."

Sorrow rushed through her thinking her only sister had missed her wedding. Yet there were plenty of days left in the wedding celebrations, weren't there?

Kitty scanned the room, hoping to introduce her king to Esther. Seeming to know she was thinking of him, Errol slipped into view from the shadows of a veranda and sauntered in their direction. His smile shined more radiant than ever. A halo of light surrounded him as though he were an angel descended from Heaven. Kitty's gaze drifted down his strong torso to what he held in his left hand. She licked her lips, her eyes latching onto the most beautiful of fruits. The pomegranate she adored, that she would relish endlessly.

Esther watched him, too, but not in the way Kitty had hoped. Her expression seemed curious, filled with something Kitty couldn't quite place. Was it terror? No, that was impossible. Who could fear such a man?

But then something clawed at that back of Kitty's mind, rising from the abyss. Before she could drag it out from the depths, Errol slowed to a stop in front of them and ran a juice-covered finger across Kitty's lips. Her eyelids fluttered as he spoke, "I received news your sister was among us. Are you now completely happy, my love?"

"Happier than ever," Kitty murmured. "You truly would do anything for me."

Errol turned to face Esther and grasped her hand in his. He lowered his head to press a kiss against her skin, his lips lingering there. "We've been waiting so long to meet you, dear Esther," he said. "My kingdom has so much to offer you." He trailed a hand down Esther's cheek and cooed, "You look very like your sister. Exquisite indeed."

"She does." Kitty grinned with pride.

Her elation slipped for a fraction as his sapphire gaze stayed pinned on her sister, hungrily. A stare that she hoped he'd only ever given to her: insatiable, lustful. The sweetness of the pomegranate slipped between Kitty's lips the next instant, and she sighed. She couldn't draw out the words or feelings that lurked inside her. Joy and pride at Errol's appreciation of her sister swelled within her.

Kitty's eyes locked on Esther's tattered blue dress, unsuitable for the occasion. "You must have a new gown to join in our celebrations. These old rags simply won't do at all."

"No," Esther said quickly. "I love this dress. You made it for me, remember?" she drew her words out slowly, as if attempting to hint at something lost.

"Back when we barely had a coin to our names." Her sister deserved much better now. "Money doesn't matter here. Something beautiful for her, Errol. Please." Kitty pulled on his arm.

"Of course." Errol smirked. He lifted a hand, and a moment later Esther's drab old dress was gone, replaced by a sparkling silver ballgown with diamond buttons. Her sister's breasts nearly spilled out of its low neckline. Esther's golden hair hung down her back in thick curls, glitter sparkled around her eyes, and crystal heels covered her feet.

Esther blinked, paling for an instant before that same fake smile returned. "It's gorgeous really," she said. "But I still preferred your dress, Kitty. Always."

"How about you pick a gentleman to dance with?" Aunt Lizzie chirped.

"Oh no, I couldn't." Esther waved her off while peering at the crowd. All the kingdom waited eagerly for a dance with Kitty's beautiful sister. "Everyone here is wearing masks. I wouldn't know how to choose amongst them."

In response, the crowd removed their masks as one, and Esther gasped, her eyes going wide.

"Everything is so wonderful here," she said. "It's still too difficult and I must admit I'm tired from my journey. Would it displease you too awfully if I sit back and watch?"

"Of course. Let's go sit together, and perhaps you can meet Nova, my new kitten, once she returns from wandering off." Kitty led Esther to one of the silk settees, but their mother stepped forward, halting their progress.

"How about him?" Their mother pointed with a grin to a man in the center of the room, the second most breathtakingly handsome in the kingdom after Errol. The man's chestnut hair was drawn back into a low ponytail and his light gray eyes were akin to a beautiful stormy sky.

Esther pinched her lips together as the man sauntered toward her.

"I've been waiting for you, Esther," he said with a bow, his voice soft.

"How can that be?" Esther arched a brow. "I don't even know your name."

"Dance with me, and I'll tell you." The man reached out, enfolding Esther's hand within his grasp. She looked as if she wanted to argue, but she didn't, allowing herself instead to be guided across the marble ballroom floor. As he spun Esther in graceful circles beneath the sparkling chandeliers and though music filled the world with a melody sweeter than honey, Kitty found it odd that not once did Esther take her eyes off her.

It made no sense! Why couldn't Esther relax and enjoy herself?

"She doesn't look content." Kitty pouted. "It's vexing, really."

Errol laughed, looping his arm around her waist and pulling her close. He turned Kitty's face to meet his gaze instead of Esther's, then held up another pomegranate. "How about you share your fruit with her? She must be incredibly hungry after her long journey."

"Oh, of course! How selfish I've been." Kitty took the fruit from the king's hand, and once the dance ceased, she approached Esther. "Eat, sister, you deserve the best food there is."

Esther studied the fruit as though it were from the snake slinking about the Garden of Eden. "I'm not hungry just yet, thank you, Kitty."

"You have to be famished by now and must eat!" Kitty held the fruit closer to Esther's lips, and her sister stepped back.

"I'll eat soon, I promise." Esther leaned close and whispered in her sister's ear, "Can we please talk alone now?"

Errol's deep, alluring voice interrupted them, "How about a dance with me, Esther?"

"Oh, no, that wouldn't be proper at all, would it?" Esther's words sounded rushed, almost panicked.

Kitty frowned.

Another dance was exactly what her sister needed. She should get to know the people she would be surrounded by, not run off to talk to Kitty alone somewhere in the shadows.

"It's only a dance, silly." Kitty beamed, kissing her king's cheek. "Errol shouldn't be a stranger to you—he's family now." She nudged her sister forward.

"You may speak to your sister alone after, if you wish," Errol said to Esther before sweeping her away to the ballroom floor.

As her husband danced with Esther, Kitty joined her mother and aunt, luxuriating in their warm embrace while all three watched, their lips curled up at the edges. But as Kitty continued to notice that Esther's fake smile never left her face, unease unraveled within her. She simply couldn't understand what was wrong. Surrounded by enchanting beauty so magical it took her breath away, what was there to fear?

Twelve

∞

ESTHER

"**A** maiden who tastes the goblins' fruit gains a mind that is no longer her own," Esther's mother explained, her eyes on the fire, her chair rocking back and forth. "She will see, hear, and feel only what those creatures wish her to. Your aunt knew she must pretend to be under their spell, that this was the only way she could save me. And she did it, the slightest misstep would have meant my destruction, but she did it."

Esther's heart was breaking.

She'd always thought the expression ridiculous. It turned out she simply never understood it, until now. Even when her father died, even when she found her mother and aunt brutally murdered, Esther's heart had persevered. She had grieved, and it had been painful. Yet it faded, the edges of grief's blades losing their sharpness, and she had started, even against her will, to heal. Witnessing Kitty's abuse in this goblin hell, her sister's beautiful mind so completely lost, her body withered and dying in her bed at home while monsters devoured her youth, Esther's hope slipped from her grasp.

Esther's mother had never been swept away by goblins this deeply when Aunt Lizzie had rescued her. Esther could not save her sister, could not help the one person she promised to always stand by, to protect with her very life. Kitty was lost, and the fact broke her heart.

We are not defeated yet, Esther told herself, sudden fury giving her strength as the crowd of goblins roared with laughter at her sister. Kitty, her clothing torn and filthy, danced around the dank and bone-strewn courtyard on bloodied feet, her smile ecstatic, her arms embracing nothing.

Pull yourself together, Esther Elizabeth Morris. The battle has only just begun.

After years of listening to her mother's stories, Esther knew from the moment Kitty appeared, she mustn't upset her sister's perfect dreamworld too suddenly. It could break her mind further or even quicken her death, leaving her soul trapped with the Goblin King.

The frailty of the human mind entertained goblins, viewing her sister as a toy easily made malleable by something as simple as their devilish fruit. Esther could see for herself the magical paradise that Kitty saw, though it was transparent to her, a shadowy illusion over the real goblin world. She could see both the monsters her sister perceived as their loving mother and aunt, and the Goblin King as Kitty's beloved, a man so exquisitely handsome it took her own breath away.

Esther needed to find a way to lift the veil of illusion from Kitty without sacrificing her. She would only turn from this world if she saw it for what it truly was.

What's the matter, darling? Aren't you happy for your sister? Esther felt ill at the memory of that voice, which had been simultaneously both her mother's and the goblin's.

Embracing the monsters wearing the faces of those she loved so dearly, while pretending joy as she did so was the hardest thing Esther had ever done.

Kitty imagined a lavish party, and Esther forced herself to play along, even letting the horrid king lead her onto the ball-room floor. But she only had so much time to free her sister from this false prison.

"We've danced enough. You said I would be able to speak to Kitty alone," she told him, smiling brightly at Kitty whose gaze never left her. She sat amongst the goblins who wore their mother and aunt's faces, absently petting a creature covered in blue scales, with eight serpents for legs and horns like twisted bones, that sat upon her lap. Its glowing red eyes watched Esther with malevolence. That must've been Nova —her *pet*.

"Did I?" the Goblin King answered absently. "Ah! So I did."

A wicked smile playing across his lips, he snapped his clawed fingers, and the illusion of a lavish party vanished. A courtyard of cold, black coal strewn with discarded carcasses appeared, empty but for the two of them. Three floors of dark windows looked down on them like vacuous eye sockets, their panes broken and jagged.

"What have you done?" Esther cried, staggering from his side. "Where is Kitty?"

The Goblin King threw his head back and laughed. The sound sent a horde of batlike creatures into flight against the crimson sky. He turned with a sweep of his filthy cloak. "You are in my domain," he cooed. "Didn't anyone ever warn you not to trust your eyes when in the company of goblins?"

"I want you to release my sister," Esther said between gritted teeth. "I'm stronger than her. Use me instead."

"In due time, you will be mine," the king purred.

"What purpose do we serve you?"

At first, Esther thought the Goblin King wouldn't answer. He gazed up at the lightning-strewn sky, his vine-covered skin crawling with shining insects, a corpse unable to decay in its grave.

But then he turned his bottomless eyes on her and when he smiled, it was as though he observed a beautiful meal.

"Everything," he said simply. "Your lives are everything to us." He spread his arms wide and tilted his crowned head back. "They give this world life. Like the air you breathe, or the water you drink. We breathe, we drink..."

Esther's throat dried. Her words hardly making a sound as she finished his sentence, "Innocent souls."

"Of a certain flavor, yes."

Esther gazed at the surroundings, as if for the first time: the pocked and cracked castle walls; the sky of blood-red and darkness above; the world's general air of ruin and decay. His goblin kingdom was dying despite the mountain of bodies outside its castle walls and the many lives the temptation of his evil fruit had claimed.

Meeting his gaze, Esther realized the Goblin King studied her intently. His head tilted like a buzzard, and a bone-chilling smile spread across his terrifying face. Esther almost wished that she only saw the beauty Kitty was ensnared by.

"My kingdom does not prosper," he said, his voice akin to thunder across the foggy moors. "Because I am merciful, we goblins only take what we need."

"I need to see my sister," Esther ground out, just barely keeping her tears at bay.

He held out his hand, a perfect pear resting in his palm,

and Esther longed to take a bite. Her body rioted against her mind as her hand itched to reach for it.

"Eat our fruit," the Goblin King purred. "Everyone does in the end. You will be no different."

She shook her head no. "You promised I could speak to my sister alone."

"Ah, yes. So I did."

Rain, like frigid needles, fell against Esther's face as she waited atop the castle's battlement alone. Not once did her gaze waver from the gaping hole in the black stone. Her heart raced in terror that her time would be up before Kitty joined her.

At last, footfalls echoed on the stone steps. Esther rushed forward, only to halt as three creatures emerged from the darkness, each more hideous than the next. The third held a rusted chain over its scaled shoulder, its beady eyes dancing with laughter while it tugged a staggering Kitty into view.

The trio burst into applause as Esther trained her reaction; she refused to look at them. Kitty's shackles were secured to the stone. Her neck and arms were held in place, and her hair hung in wet tendrils across her oblivious, smiling face. Somehow, she was still beautiful.

"Esther!" she said brightly, and Esther let the mirage of her sister's arms encircling her in warm welcome fall across her vision, a blessed reprieve from reality's horror. "We are alone at last, just as you wished."

The trio of goblins retreated down the stairs, their cackles fading, and Esther closed her eyes with a sigh. When she opened them again, she saw everything as Kitty did.

A bedchamber of unimaginable luxury replaced the watery battlement. The collar of steel around Kitty's neck became a strand of pearls the size of grapes. Her rags transformed into a gown of silk and lace a shade of lavender never achieved by human hands, her torn feet encased in fur-lined slippers. A deliciously warm fire crackled within a marble fireplace the size of Esther's entire bedroom back home.

Oh, if only this were real, Esther thought.

Kitty's smile vanished and she frowned, turning to the bowl of fruit. Esther realized with a jolt of fear this was not part of the illusion. "Why aren't you eating? Isn't the food to your liking? I can promise it's more delicious than anything our world has to offer."

"Oh, I did eat already. Thank you, Kitty," Esther said, praying her smile looked genuine. "I ate so much right before you entered, really, I couldn't eat another bite tonight."

Kitty stilled, her gaze narrowing in suspicion.

"The plums were my favorite," Esther hurried on. "Absolutely divine. And the pears! Honestly, I could eat and eat this fruit forever and never stop, but sleep threatened to overtake me. I thought I might finish in the morning."

Maybe if I can get those shackles off her, Kitty will see, Esther thought, grasping for her sister. *But what can I say to wake her? How can I show her that what she sees isn't real and convince her to come home with me?* Esther remembered the Goblin King feeding Kitty, and a spark of hope awakened as an idea came to her. *Perhaps if she abstains from their fruit for long enough, she will see, yet how can I keep her from eating it?*

As if in answer, Kitty reached for the fruit within her shackled hand, the illusion and reality flashing in odd juxtaposition. Rain slowly filled the golden platter. The tantalizing grapes and apples sparkled with moisture, and Esther snatched the bowl from Kitty.

For an instant, Kitty's eyes filled with panic and rage, as if tasting the goblin fruit was all she desired. But then she blinked at Esther and smiled, confusion replacing rage.

"Oh, of course." She laughed lightly. "How rude of me. I've become so greedy, haven't I? One would never guess by my gluttony that I have more than enough in my bedchamber."

Silence filled the room, the sound of rain on stone fading as Esther studied her sister, daring to hope.

Was that a flash of fear in Kitty's eyes? Was she seeing the goblin realm for what it was, even if only for an instant? Embracing her sister, Esther rushed to unfasten her shackles, letting the collar of steel fall to the stone. She took Kitty's hands in hers, freeing her bruised wrists from chains.

Yes. There. Esther was sure that Kitty felt the rain for the first time. And there! She startled when lightning flashed across the sky.

"Esther...?" Kitty shook her head, paling.

"Come home with me," Esther pleaded, praying this wouldn't break Kitty's mind. "You are dying, my sweet sister. Come home. We can find a way to make you well again, just as Aunt Lizzie did for Mother, all those years ago. I know we can."

Kitty trembled, shivering in the driving rain, and when her eyes met Esther's, they were clear. For a heartbeat, Esther thought it had worked, that Kitty would come with her, that her beautiful mind was restored.

But then, like a veil falling between them, Kitty's gaze unfocused.

"Oh, my dear Esther, don't worry," she gasped, hugging

Esther fiercely. "I will help you become well. Here." Kitty's mirage of heaven consumed the watery battlement once again.

Esther watched in dismay, helpless to stop her when Kitty spun from her grasp and fled for the doors, her voice overflowing with grief and terror as she screamed into the opulent hallway beyond, "Help! Please, somebody help! Guards! We need a doctor for my sister!" And then by wicked magic, Kitty vanished into thin air.

Familiar laughter filled the night, and Esther turned to see the Goblin King perched atop the castle parapet like a giant bat, slowly clapping his hands.

"Take her away," he ordered in a voice cold as ice. Esther's own screams filled the night as creatures enclosed her from every angle. They dragged her into the darkness of the stairwell.

Her heart wasn't breaking. It was shattered to pieces.

Thirteen

KITTY

Kitty sobbed into her hands. Why was her sister being like this? Why wasn't she graciously accepting the gifts she'd been blessed with?

Esther suffered from hysteria. The fact could no longer be denied. There was no other possible explanation for her behavior. She'd refused to eat the delicious fruit that held miraculous properties. Properties that would heal her from all torment and pain. Kitty couldn't stop thinking about how Esther had lied—her stomach was empty, not filled. Her sister hadn't touched the platter of fruit in her room, much less taken a single bite. It made no sense! Esther had always loved fruit, would sneak bites from the apples and berries when making pies. Never was she full enough to refuse a slice, even when their...their...

Kitty couldn't remember how to finish her thought. But it didn't matter—she would make certain her sister ate, that she became healthy once more, and they would live happily together, enjoying every luxury offered to them.

She recalled rumors of a female villager in her old world who was whispered to be suffering from hysteria, how the very idea had been shameful, something to keep quiet about. There were articles in the Sunday papers about it last summer. Women in the cities were hauled away to asylums—*madhouses*—and never heard from again.

Kitty shrugged off the horrid thought. This caring and beautiful world's laws were nothing of that sort. King Errol would help Kitty cure her sister and bring her back to glowing health, not toss her away like refuse.

Kitty lowered her hands to her sides and peered at her surroundings. She was no longer in one of the spare rooms but in her garden. She stared up at the starlit sky. Faeries laughed and fluttered beneath the moon, their skin sparkling like jewels, their wings iridescent lace. Lanterns had been placed along a mossy trail between fields of foxglove and primrose, and Kitty's gaze followed it toward a shadowy figure. The figure stepped forward into the flickering glow, and Kitty's breath caught.

Errol bit his lip, and loving concern filled his expression as he swiftly approached her. When he was only a hair's breadth from her, he gathered her hands in his and murmured, "Esther is receiving the best of care just down the hall from our room. I'm so sorry, my queen, this entire ordeal must be unimaginably trying for you."

Kitty collapsed before him and clutched his thighs, worry for Esther overtaking her. "Promise me you won't take her away, that she won't be thrown into an asylum?" She knew in her heart he would never do such a thing, but she had to hear it from his lips.

Errol dropped in front of her like a true knight, a king

before his queen, and cupped her cheek. "Whyever would I do anything of such a dishonorable nature? Do you believe me to be a monster?" Hurt lingered in his voice, his expression turning melancholic.

Guilt churned within her, and Kitty threw her arms around him, holding him close. "Of course not. I would never believe you monstrous." Hot tears pricked her eyes, and she nuzzled his neck, breathing in his apple scent. "I shouldn't have left Esther, and here I am hiding away from her in the garden. I must go to her at once and remain at her side until she is well."

Errol tilted Kitty's chin so their gazes met, his voice low and calm as he spoke, "That is something you cannot do, my love. No matter how much you or I wish it possible. You must sleep as well. But fear not. While you rest, I will have someone sit with sweet Esther. They will treat her as a sibling. She is already like a sister to me."

Kitty smiled, gratitude flooding her heart as she wiped her cheeks and stood. "You truly are a gift from God, my king. No one else would've accepted my sister with open arms as you have, especially now that she is ill. Thank you." She drew his face to hers and pressed her lips tenderly to his, tasting delicious apples that matched his calming scent.

As she stepped back, a golden bowl of blueberries awaited her in his palm, his other hand tenderly stroking her cheek. "For your own health, eat before visiting her. You wouldn't want to starve yourself too, and what you don't finish, offer to Esther. Perhaps she'll be willing to eat this time."

So thoughtful...

Kitty nodded and placed a velvety blueberry on her

tongue. She chewed it slowly, savoring the juice as it drizzled down her throat, delighting in the newfound strength that washed over her.

"I do believe you're right." She would get the sister she knew back, the one who would fight to live. The one who knew that regaining her health meant she must nourish her body with wholesome sustenance—not starve it.

Kitty ate two more blueberries and a kaleidoscope of golden butterflies swarmed above her. She absorbed the moment of peace before Errol clasped her hand and led her from the garden back into the palace. His strong presence was a comfort as they approached Esther's door, where raging screams vibrated the walls. Kitty's stomach sank at the desperate sounds.

Breathing deeply, she untangled her fingers from Errol's, hesitant to let him go. "I would like to visit Esther alone, if that is all right?"

The last time the sisters were by themselves it hadn't gone well, but perhaps this time things would be different.

He kissed her knuckles, soothing her. "Of course, my love. But if you need me, just call my name and I'll be wherever you wish."

As Errol strode away from her, Kitty opened the door and gasped. Esther sat bound to a golden chair, her wrists tied with velvet rope as she shrieked and writhed like a wild badger caught in a trap.

Esther's gaze met Kitty's and she stilled, relief filling her face. "Sister," she panted. "Untie me immediately."

"You mustn't test yourself, Esther. Try to remain calm," Kitty said gently. "We have to trust the physicians—they will make you well."

Kitty sank to the floor beside her sister and lay her head

in Esther's lap just as she used to when they were little. Her sister would run her fingers through Kitty's tangled curls, and whatever terrible thing happened that day would fade away.

Only now, Esther couldn't move, and Kitty wouldn't loosen the binds to free her hands. She would not risk her sister hurting herself further.

The infirmary room was an enchanting dream, so why didn't her sister smile even a little? Doves of pure white danced above them. Hummingbirds drank nectar from honeysuckle blooming along the vines hanging from every window. The ceiling was nothing but summer sky.

A bed fit for a princess, draped in satin sheets, awaited Esther, if only she would stop struggling against her treatment. At least her chair was made of the most comfortable velvet—only a small taste of what luxury she could enjoy if she would just eat.

"Kitty," Esther groaned. "I didn't want to alarm you, but you must *listen* to me. Please, we're running out of time."

"I am listening," Kitty told her. Oh, it was terrible to see Esther this way, her eyes that of a mad woman.

"You aren't really here, and neither am I," Esther whispered. "You're at our house, Kitty. Our mother's house. I went to a witch so that I could come here and help you because you're dying. Do you understand?"

No. No, no, no! Esther was delusional. But she could be well again, so easily. If only she ate!

Kitty lifted a plump blueberry from the golden bowl and held it up to her sister's mouth. Esther twisted away from the fruit as if it might scald her, clamping her lips so that none of the precious fruit touched even one tastebud.

Annoyance and desperation clawed at Kitty. Why was

Esther being so impossible? Her behavior was insufferable. She would rather die than eat? Did she not trust Kitty, who had told her repeatedly that this fruit would help make her well—even better than well? It was too much to bear.

"Eat!" Kitty screamed. At her wits end, she finally attempted to force the fruit into Esther's mouth. To no avail.

Kitty was unable to hold her panic in check, and falling to her knees, she pleaded with Esther, "You must eat, or you'll die!"

Esther blinked, and pity shone in her stare. "Listen to me first, Kitty. And then we'll discuss the fruit. I promise."

Kitty nodded, willing to do anything to get her older sister to accept the blueberry.

"Think as hard as you can, and don't speak," Esther continued. "Remember Mother and Aunt Lizzie's stories?"

Kitty furrowed her brow, concentrating, but nothing came to mind. She searched her memory for what her sister was describing yet could remember nothing. They hadn't ever been told stories...

"Mother and Aunt Lizzie won against the goblins," Esther whispered. "Though they didn't really, did they? Because the goblins came back and murdered them. But that wasn't the end of their vengeance. They came for you, and now they're trying to take my life as well. This place, this palace, it belongs to the goblins. None of what your eyes are observing is truly real, don't you see? It's inside your mind, a heaven of luxury, love, and adoration keeping you complacent and happy while your body is left behind to decay and die. And once you die, they'll have your soul.

"I traveled here, into your thoughts, yet I can still see this place for what it is. Nothing is as you believe it to be. That husband of yours is not a human man at all. He's the Goblin

King, a *monster*. He's grotesque, wicked, and hellbent on destroying you and me."

Her mind is lost completely, Kitty realized with a jolt of horror. *What devilish plot has her insanity concocted that she would say such vile and cruel things?*

"Lies!" Kitty hissed, shrinking away from her sister in disgust and pity. "You are mad. Mad beyond belief. You must stop speaking these falsehoods." How could Esther say such things? Why would she purposefully try to hurt Kitty? No. This wasn't the sister she knew at all.

"No, Kitty, you must listen." Esther straightened in her seat, anguish filling her eyes. "Stop eating their fruit, and you will see that I speak truth! You will heal and you will come back to me. Please, you must try, for God's sake, please just try."

One thing was clear at least: Esther believed her own twisted and grotesque lies.

"No." Kitty's breaths grew ragged, her chest heaving. "No. Eat and *you* will see!"

"I will not." Esther shook her head. "Now think, Kitty! This isn't you. You are strong, and you are brave, and you wouldn't fall in love so quickly, would you? Remember Duncan? Your eyes always lit up when you saw him. He's watching over you now and promised to take you to a village dance if you would just wake. Let's go back, and we can be a family again."

Duncan? Kitty had never heard such a ridiculous name, nor had she ever found anyone attractive except for her king.

Kitty realized what was happening. She knew precisely why Esther was acting this way. "You're just jealous of the love between me and Errol. I understand he isn't a possible choice, but the man you danced with has already fallen for you. He can be your sunshine too."

Esther winced, then whispered, "I'll get you home, Kitty. I promise."

The door opened and Kitty whirled around to find a tall, thin man in a dark suit, his bright red hair hanging in disarray around his face.

"I'm the healer," he said hurriedly, rushing toward them. "King Errol sent me to help your sister."

"Stay away from me!" Esther spat as the healer stepped beside her and opened his satchel. "Kitty, remember who you are!"

But Kitty already knew who she was. Esther was the one who'd forgotten, who'd lost her sanity.

The healer sprinkled iridescent powder onto Esther's sweat-slicked forehead and studied her eyes before sighing. He turned back to Kitty, calm even as Esther continued to spew nonsense.

"There are a couple of things we can try," he murmured, his eyes full of sympathy. "But I believe we should start simple first. I can perform bloodletting and allow Esther's body to weaken until she desires to consume food."

Kitty sucked in a sharp breath. "What if she bleeds too much?"

Hadn't she heard of patients who had bled and bled until they died?

"On my honor as the king's loyal healer, I will not let that happen. But for now, I would like you to take comfort somewhere else while I begin treatment." He ushered her toward the door, and Kitty ignored the gesture. "If you stay, it will only upset you and the patient, I'm afraid."

Kitty mulled this over while holding back the urge to

protest. The task didn't seem as terrifying as some of the things she'd read about in medical tomes at the library: induced vomiting and diarrhea, along with the bloodletting; drills and nails through the skull to cure the brain; scandalously, *unthinkable*, pelvic massages to lessen hysteria.

"I trust you'll take care of my sister as though she were your own," Kitty finally said. "But I don't want to leave her alone."

Esther shouted louder. "Don't go, Kitty! Don't listen to this bastard. Don't listen to *anyone*!"

"You're only making her more hysterical. Please, for your sister's safety, come back in the morning. And in the meantime, trust that I will be doing everything I can for her," the healer promised.

Esther rattled the chair harder, and if it hadn't been weighted, it would've toppled over. "Kitty, you mustn't eat the fruit! You'll see that I'm right if you only stop eating!"

The doctor retrieved a leather belt from his satchel and calmly placed it between Esther's lips as she snapped at his fingertips. "I'm sorry, Majesty, but I must do this." He sighed. "Really, it's for her own good."

Tears stung Kitty's eyes, but she prepared to do as she was told. For Esther. "I love you more than anything, sister," she said. "And I will do everything in my power to save you, even if you hate me for it. I vow to return to you in the morning." With that, Kitty fled the room and rushed into her own bedchamber.

Nova awaited her at the desk and rubbed her furry body against Kitty's leg, purring. She petted the kitten's head before throwing herself on the bed and curling her knees into her chest. There had been mournful moments in her life, although...she couldn't recall a single one now. Perhaps there hadn't been sadness in her life at all. This was the first distress she'd ever suffered from. She'd only ever been blessed with happiness. At the memory of Esther's screams, her hurtful lies, Kitty's heart felt as though it would burst, that she would dissolve into nothing. There was only one person who could help her from splitting into pieces.

"Errol, I need you!" she called through choked sobs.

And when she raised her head from the pillow, the king stood beside her. His hair hung in neat sheets down his bare chest, a basket of strawberries in his grasp. He sat beside her and lifted Kitty into his lap. She gladly rested her head against his shoulder, enveloped in his warm embrace as she cried.

He fed her strawberry after strawberry until her tears vanished.

Eventually, silence stretched throughout the room, and Errol tilted Kitty's chin to face him, his brilliant eyes blazing with yearning. "Do you want my love? My touch? I ache for nothing more than to make you feel better."

His love. It was the only thing that could help her, that could take away all her pain.

"Yes," she answered, her voice breathy. "Make our clothing disappear. Take away this suffering."

Errol's lips caressed hers, tasting of the most luscious of nectarines, and she melted at his touch. As if she weighed nothing at all, he turned her in his lap so that her legs cradled his thighs, and their clothing was gone. His hands caressed her skin while he whispered sweet nothings into her ear and promised her a lifetime of happiness. No more pain.

And she believed him.

Kitty's eyelids fluttered when she grew suddenly tired, a deeply rooted exhaustion spreading from her fingers to her toes. Her muscles and skin ached as though her youth were gone, leaving her an old woman with creaking, aching bones.

Images of apples surrounded her, their lush bodies withering, worms snaking in and out of their rotting forms. Unable to gather strength to speak, she sank deeper into a world of rot, holding on to the fact that in the morning Esther would be healed when Kitty woke back into her perfect world.

Fourteen

ESTHER

Esther's cell door creaked open, and the Goblin King prowled in. Something in his smug expression told Esther he'd had his way with her sister, and she wanted to slice into his skin with burning knives and never stop. But even though she was no longer bound to the chair, her legs and arms were now tied.

Errol's boots halted in front of her, and he glowered down at her as she lay panting against the filthy stone. His bottomless eyes studied her as if she were a curiosity in a freakshow.

"Where is Kitty?" Esther struggled to ask through the leather strap between her teeth.

The monstrous healer stood in the corner watching them. Once Kitty had left, he'd continued to study her as though she were a specimen, poking at her throat and abdomen with his bony fingers before fiddling with artificial leeches and a hernia tool, to which, praise God, he hadn't used on her yet.

The Goblin King answered, "She's alive, and that is all

you need to know. *Now*, you can either willingly eat a piece of fruit," he drawled, then shrugged. "Or we can take a little trip to the dungeons until you change your mind." He motioned, and the belt vanished from her mouth, along with the ropes around her wrists and ankles.

Esther pursed her lips, understanding she could not become his unless she took a bite of her own accord. "I will not eat your fruit unless you give up my sister."

"I don't bargain with humans."

It was no use. Kitty remained now and forever lost to her, despite her best efforts.

"Please." Her throat felt as though it were on fire, torn and raw with screaming, her limbs trembling and weak from struggle.

"No."

As she shoved up from the floor, Errol pushed her back down. Esther's neck twisted at a painful angle when the Goblin King's cold fingers clenched her jaw, forcing her to face him. With his savage gaze only inches from hers, the stench of rot and sulphur radiated off him. Two golden stag beetles crawled from his mouth, traveling up his cheek. Despair at her failure drowned her mind.

"Do *not* defy me," he growled.

Esther wrenched her chin from his grasp. "You do not have my soul."

He rose, a vicious smile spreading across his face. "The dungeons it is, then."

Esther blinked and found herself transported to a rowboat. The Goblin King sat calmly beside her, his gaze on the clearing mist. The *healer* was no longer with them. A silent cloaked figure guided the weathered craft toward the looming castle. A hole like a screaming mouth grew closer as the boat slid across stagnant water, its murky depths putrid with rot, the stench of death wafting across its surface.

As they entered the corridor, the Goblin King waved a languid hand, and torches came to life, illuminating their way. Esther gasped as bile threatened to choke her.

"Lovely, isn't it?" His dark laughter chilled her to the bone.

Esther's traitorous eyes soaked in every detail of her surroundings while the boat floated between columns of the dead and the dying. Bleeding creatures stood on display, held up only by the stakes that impaled them. Most merely blinked unseeing eyes, a few watching her with crazed hope, their screams unintelligible. Still more creatures floated above them like grotesque lanterns, imprisoned in cages. Their cries for water grew in volume as the boat drew near, until they screamed for mercy.

"And what method would you choose?" the king asked, his tone light, akin to inquiring how many sugars she took with her tea. "If you could select from our extensive menu yourself, what would you have?"

Esther's mind revolted against the very thought of his dungeon's *extensive menu*, and she said nothing.

"Oh, how discourteous of me," he continued, as if Esther weren't about to be sick when they passed beneath two men who looked human except for their pointed ears and striped skin. They were hung on either side of the castle's watery entrance like blood-soaked angels of Hell, their ribs ripped out of their backs, spread wide like wings. Blood painted their bodies and legs crimson, their pale faces frozen in death.

"That method is known as The Bloody Eagle." He pointed a clawed finger. "Nasty way to go, but fast. That"—he jerked his chin at what appeared at first to be a display in a butcher shop—arms, legs, and torso nothing more than strips of bloody and torn meat—"is a slower method. It turns out that skin can be pulled from muscle rather easily, provided one cooks the offender a bit first."

Esther nearly fell out of the boat as one of the things hanging bloody and skinless from the cavernous ceiling shrieked in agony, and the Goblin King chuckled.

The cavern's enormous entrance hall stretched on and on, a lightless passage off to the right filling with water as the tide rose. Their silent captain guided the craft along a fetid river that wound like a rotting serpent toward crumbling stairs of ebony. Esther thought surely, *surely* three hours must've passed by now. Did time move differently here in this hell? Did one minute feel to the mind like an entire eternity? That was something she couldn't recall being in her mother or aunt's stories.

Had the witch lied to her about being able to return to her world? She trembled at the thought, but determined not to beg for her life, no matter what dreadful things they did to her, or how many beatings their *healer* administered. If the Goblin King had her soul, she would be worthless to help Kitty and her sister would assuredly be doomed.

Reaching the staircase, the Goblin King stepped from the boat and offered Esther his hand. When she refused it, she found herself standing by his side, his laughter filling the cavernous space akin to nails in a coffin.

"You are in my world," he cooed. "You cannot escape my will."

I have not eaten your fruit yet, Esther thought. *I still see you for what you are. I still see the truth.*

The Goblin King strode forward with a sweep of his cloak, and Esther found she was powerless against him. She stayed by his side, seeming to be held in place by invisible chains. He watched her hungrily as though he wanted to taste her youth the way she knew he had her sister's.

The stairways steepened, and she knew they were now beneath the castle. Screams echoed, a symphony of pain and dying creatures, the air as cold as ice. Room after room displayed horrors of which Esther knew she would never recover from the sight of.

"Ah, this one is deliciously wicked," he told her as a male creature lay tied to a stone slab with ropes of leather. A metal can of sorts hung above his face, and as Esther watched, she noticed tiny drops of water falling to hit his blistered forehead, each one making him cry out in pain. "At first, the water is merely an annoyance. But water is powerful enough to erode stone, and soon his skin will blister, then tear open, until eventually those tiny droplets drill a hole right into his skull."

Esther refused to speak, though he seemed to wait eagerly for a response.

"One more." The Goblin King sounded cross now. "And then you will choose to eat the fruit or not."

Heat permeated from the next room, and Esther was nearly grateful for the warmth against her numb hands and face. A creature of strange beauty lay naked on a slab of stone, a clay bowl placed against his groin, his wrists and ankles tied, limbs stretched wide.

"That bowl," the Goblin King whispered, "holds a particularly large rat. Do pay attention."

Esther held back a cry as a hooded figure entered the room and heated the clay vessel with red-hot clamps. Soon the male screamed as the animal within struggled to escape its burning prison, digging into his skin.

"Some have actually survived this," the Goblin King murmured, his lips against Esther's cheek. "Provided the rat doesn't chew through anything vital, it's possible to be left with nothing more than a nasty scar. Does this entice you to accept my fruit?"

"Do what you will with me," Esther said. "I will not eat your wicked fruit." This monster had taken everything from her—he would not take her soul for nothing. For Kitty's life, she would give it up, allowing him to do what he wished to her.

"A pity." He squeezed her arm, and Esther found herself transported once again.

Everything was white: white walls, white floor, white chairs, white bed, white door. The light in the room was brighter than anything Esther had ever experienced.

"Few survive the white room," the Goblin King drawled, his voice filling the space. "Most choose to take their own lives, and those who make it out alive are never the same again." With a devious smile, a bright red apple appeared in his palm. Esther's dry mouth begged for one taste, for its juice to take her thirst away. She shakily reached for the goblin's fruit, then yanked her hand away from it.

Please, God, Esther prayed, her tiny spark of hope surprising even herself. *Deliver us from this evil.*

"If you don't eat the apple, you will suffer the full effects of my wrath."

"So be it," Esther said, lifting her chin in defiance. "Do your worst to me. Or give up my sister and I'll eat it."

Esther found that she lay splayed against the white bed, unable to move, unable to close her eyes against the room's unrelenting brightness. It appeared simpler than anything the Goblin King had shown her, only it wasn't. Everything about the striking white pierced each of her senses like nails through her flesh.

She remained there for what felt like hours, until her eyes were as dry as marbles. Until she was sure she would go mad. Until, God help her, her mind begged for death.

And then something red hovered above her—the forsaken apple. She bit her tongue, her body quaking for one, single lush bite.

A shadow fell across her vision. A hooded figure loomed over her; its face hidden in darkness. It raised its arms, and Esther saw with horror that it had curved metal claws instead of fingers. There had to be another way to get out of this, to save her sister. *There had to be.*

"It's time we rearranged those organs, yes?" The Goblin King's laughter echoed throughout the dungeon. "Perhaps the loss of blood will bring you to your senses."

Agony that Esther could not have ever imagined permeated her torso, radiating along her every nerve, pain filling her mind to bursting. But even as screams tore from her throat, Esther didn't give in to the fruit.

Instead, she woke.

Esther peered at Duncan's wild eyes, then the clock on the wall—three hours had passed. She lay in her own room, Kitty, barely alive now, by her side. Sitting with a gasp, the Goblin King's laughter still ringing in her ears, Esther knew at last what she must do to save her sister.

Fifteen

KITTY

itty, I'm coming back for you.

Cool wind blew across Kitty's face, and she jolted awake, shivering. Gooseflesh prickled her skin. Drawing the blanket up around her naked chest, she studied her surroundings. She was in her bedchamber at the palace, but Errol was nowhere to be seen. Her palm brushed the spot where he'd lain, the sheets no longer warm. However, a bowl of red currants had been left for her.

Kitty's temples throbbed. She tried to thread her thoughts together, but they resembled nothing coherent. A small furry shadow hopped on the edge of the bed, prowling toward her. The black color faded to sapphire blue. Nova licked Kitty's cheek with an urgent mewl, and she knew the kitten was telling her she needed to stop lingering in bed and start the day. Nova nudged at the fruit bowl, enticing her to pluck one.

As Kitty lifted a glistening red currant to her lips, she paused. Drifting thoughts merged, collided, then fell apart again. Esther's desperate, panic-filled voice pierced her skull, pleading with her not to eat the fruit in this world, that it belonged to *goblins*. Mad words.

If Kitty didn't eat the fruit, she would be starving herself in the same way her sister was. Perhaps Esther uttered the nonsense to lure Kitty back to their old home. It would be a deceitful thing of her to do if so, and deceitful was a quality that Esther had never held.

Kitty's hand trembled as she stared at the fruit, begging her to taste its ripe flesh, to fill her mouth with its sweet nectar. Nova released another soft meow and batted at Kitty's hand, pushing it toward her mouth. She had to prove Esther wrong, make her see that they both needed to eat to survive, to truly *live* at last. Kitty placed the red currant between her desperate lips and sighed at the heavenly taste.

Morning light spilled through the window, reminding her that there was something she must do. But everything could wait as Kitty devoured half the bowl of fruit. She recalled Errol's pleasure the night before—his warm breath, his exquisite touch, his celestial kisses. How it had... temporarily taken away the pain of... What was it? No, *who* was it? *Esther.* She remembered now. Esther was being healed and would have gone through bloodletting during the rest of the day and evening. She stopped herself from reaching for another currant.

"Esther will need these," she told herself, proud of her presence of mind at last. "You can't be selfish, Kitty."

Tossing the blankets off the bed, Kitty snatched the first dress from the wardrobe and tugged on the silky cerulean gown. She didn't bother to search for a pair of slippers as she grabbed the fruit bowl along with Nova before rushing for the door.

"You haven't gotten a chance to properly meet my sister,"

she chirped to Nova. "Perhaps holding you will make her smile."

The kitten perked up in Kitty's arm, her wide eyes beaming.

In the hallway, not a single servant passed by. The flames inside the sconces sang a crackling song while their smoke caressed the glass. Kitty leaned against the unlocked door and slowly peeked her head inside the sickroom.

"Sister, I hope you're feeling better and are not too terribly angry with me," she said softly. "I brought you two things to barter for your forgiveness."

But as her gaze swept through the room, she froze, letting the door fall open. The room was utterly empty.

No Esther. No healer. No sign that anyone had ever been there at all.

Heart thrumming, Kitty set Nova on the plush carpet, then rushed to the chair where Esther had been bound. Why hadn't anyone retrieved Kitty to inform her of Esther being transferred? No, she was worrying for nothing. The bloodletting must've been successful, and her sister was healed, walking around the palace, enjoying her morning after eating a hearty breakfast. Perhaps this happy news was meant to be a surprise for Kitty.

She hurried out of the room and took Nova and the fruit back to her bedchamber. "You'll meet my sister after your morning nap," she promised the kitten, and clutching her skirts, Kitty bolted down the grand staircase.

No guests awaited her presence for the next celebration, it being still early in the day, but her mother and Aunt Lizzie stood in a corner. They whispered to one another while holding glasses of ruby wine, both dressed in fine pearlescent gowns. The women glanced toward Kitty at the same time.

Their murmurs ceased, wide smiles forming on their smooth faces.

Too smooth...

Waxy...

Kitty blinked, and her imagination cleared. *You should've gotten more rest last night.* She searched the room, looking for her sister.

"Have either of you seen Esther? Is she healed?"

Her mother walked across the room. The golden heels she wore clicked atop the clear glass floor, a tropical garden beneath its shimmering surface. She pressed a hand to Kitty's shoulder, and the edges of her lips pulled into a frown.

"I apologize for being the bearer of unfortunate news, dearest. But Esther refused her treatment and has left us."

"No." Kitty stumbled backward, clasping a hand over her mouth. It couldn't be true. Esther would never leave without saying goodbye. "Please, bring her back again. I must speak with her at once."

"That's impossible," Aunt Lizzie said gently. "If she wants to return, she needs to come of her own accord."

Kitty thought there was something else hidden beneath their concern. Aunt Lizzie fought a smile.

"I can get her to return to this world. I know I can." Kitty's voice rose an octave and she was afraid she sounded hysterical. "I'll go myself. I'll risk my life if I have to." Even if she couldn't return here to this world as Errol had said, her sister deserved happiness.

Mother and Aunt Lizzie shook their heads with sympathy, but as they did, their faces caught the light beneath the flickering candles of the chandelier and Kitty gasped.

What stood before her was not her mother and aunt at all, but instead hideous *creatures*.

Nearly tripping over her feet while backing away, Kitty struggled to comprehend when the image of her beloved mother and aunt were drawn back into place, as if masks had been lowered over those horrible faces.

The waxiness...

The flash of monstrous features, eyes mirroring serpents', rows of teeth beneath hooked beaklike noses, their flesh couldn't be a costume. Could it?

Esther's words floated back into Kitty's mind. The holes in her memory, insanity spreading inside Kitty's skull, did not allow her to string logical information together. Something wasn't right here...

What of Errol? Kitty stared down at the tattoo encircling her finger. He was the king here. He had to have known of this deception.

Oh, good God in Heaven. Was there a mask concealing his face too?

Kitty was trapped in a nightmare of illusion.

Esther had not gone mad—she was telling the truth.

Her mother, this woman, this *thing* wearing her loved one's face, reached out for her, and Kitty recoiled from its grasp and fled.

She threw open the front door of the palace, then ran across the bridge. Kitty would find Esther and beg her sister to forgive her. She would listen this time. There was no possible way she could keep living within a false reality, seeing only what she wished to see. Esther could help mend her brain. Kitty was the insane one, not her sister, and it was...

What was it that was making her act this way? Esther's words came back to her once more. The fruit!

Wind crashed into her, as if meant to drag her back into the palace. Kitty pushed against it with all her might while racing across the meadow toward the forest. Determination thrummed within her. She must get back to her true home or die trying.

Only when she stepped into the forest, it vanished. Instead, Kitty stood within the garden Errol had gifted to her.

"No!" Kitty screeched, looking in horror at the foliage around her, searching in vain for another way to the forest. Even the door that led back into the palace had disappeared. The flowering trees rustled with the wind.

"Esther! Stay where you are!" Kitty screamed into the void. "If you can hear me, don't come to me again! I'm sorry I didn't listen to you! I'm so sorry!"

The garden stilled, the trees' limbs halting. Behind her, the sound of splashing water filled the air. Slowly turning around, Kitty saw a sparkling, pale pink lake adorned the garden's center. On its glistening surface, a gondola sailed in her direction, guided by a man wearing a golden cloak, his dark hair hanging silkily down his shoulders and back. He stood tall, regal—Errol.

The Goblin King.

She could run, but she could never hide. No matter that he rode in a boat and her feet were planted on land. He would always catch up to her, appearing wherever she went like a shadow attached to her heels.

Just as he had done in her home when he slaughtered her mother.

Tears filled Kitty's eyes when she remembered her mother's slain body, recalled how her aunt's head had rested in her own hands.

"You *monster*!" Kitty screamed. "Stay away from me! I will never eat your vile fruit again."

Even though there was nowhere to go, she spun around and fled, dodging through the flowering trees, drifting deeper into their depths. Trickles of laughter spilled from within the trunks as tiny decaying creatures watched her.

If only this were a nightmare. If only she hadn't been so foolish, drunk, and half-witted as to believe her mother had still been alive at the market that day. If only she'd realized it had been a goblin in disguise offering her the devil's fruit.

Esther.

Kitty's thoughts melded together, her self-loathing choking her as she ran. Tears streamed hot against her cheeks.

A form appeared in front of her, and Kitty was tossed violently to the ground. Hovering above her was a creature straight from Hell. A hideous beast, worse than any nightmare. Its rotting skin crawled with vines and insects, its fangs as sharp as broken glass, and it held black bottomless eyes like an endless night.

This was Errol—The Goblin King. And he'd brought her to his bed, taken pieces of her youth with every encounter, then pleasured her as she begged him for more. Nausea churned Kitty's stomach when he reached one clawed hand, fast as a viper, and forced a vial of liquid down her throat. Syrupy sweet juice slipped through her lips, filling her mouth.

"No," Kitty pleaded, choking. "I want to go home!"

"I need to feed soon," he growled. "Your essence tastes delicious, even more so than your body."

She writhed in sheer panic, her mind searching for escape. Kitty told herself that this must truly be a nightmare, that she would wake soon. She closed her eyes, then would open them to find she was at home with her sister, and their mother and aunt were still alive.

Yet when Kitty opened her eyes, she no longer stood in the middle of the garden—instead the flat bottom of a gondola swayed under her feet. Before she could think, a cold hand clamped around her throat from behind her.

"Now, now, darling," the Goblin King said. His voice sounded nothing like the one she had so loved mere hours ago. "Do stop making a fuss."

He shoved another vial of sickeningly sweet liquid into her mouth. It was like a waterfall, liquid that kept falling on and on and wouldn't end until she couldn't stop herself from giving into it. She swallowed the sweet liquid, her body, her very soul needing more.

Kitty ceased squirming against Errol's grasp and drank.

Yet, tears continued down her cheeks. Why was she crying?

The hand around her throat released its iron grip, and Kitty closed her eyes. Velvety soft fingers gently wiped the tears from her cheeks. When she looked up, a form stepped in front of her. Errol—her beautiful husband—stood before her, smiling with an adoration that made her heart ache for him.

Kitty's eyelids fluttered as she took a deep breath. "Where am I?" Was this real? How had she gotten on this gondola?

"You're with me of course." Errol's smile was as sweet as a ripe plum dipped in sugar. "Don't you remember, darling? I promised to take you for a morning boat ride before we spend another day celebrating."

Kitty swayed and Errol grasped her shoulders, holding her steady.

Oh yes, I remember now.

"How silly of me. It's such a beautiful day, and I must've fallen asleep in the sun's comfort," Kitty said, giggling as

Errol tucked one of her curls behind her ear and kissed her cheek. "Yesterday, Esther came to visit, then decided to go back home to attend to a few things. She hugged me goodbye and promised she would return soon."

"That's right," Errol purred while lifting her chin and leaning in close. "So there's nothing for my lovely queen to worry about any longer, is there?"

Something wet streaked her cheeks, and Kitty frowned, touching her face. She didn't understand why her skin wasn't dry.

Errol brushed a few droplets from beneath her eyes and smiled up at the sky. "It's raining, Kitty darling, that's all."

"Oh," Kitty murmured. "I do so love the rain."

The gondola drifted over the lake's glassy surface, its pink depths reflecting the golden sky above. Rainbows painted the air in colorful arcs. Warm rain fell gently against lotus flowers; water droplets like crystals sparkled against their pink and white petals. Kitty wrapped her arms tightly around Errol's waist and her head fell against his chest with a contented sigh.

Sixteen

ESTHER

Death came for everyone, in the end. Esther could easily spend days, weeks, even entire years ruminating over every action, word, and thought she regretted, fretting about the things she would do differently, given the chance. But after all, it was true that time moved relentlessly in one direction. A moment, once lived, was gone forever.

It was futile to dwell on life's regrets.

Especially at the end.

Esther sent Duncan home with a goodbye, a goodbye that he didn't know would be their last. But he would go on, continue to grow into an even better man, and although he wouldn't marry Kitty one day as Esther had hoped, he would eventually find someone who made him happy.

She sat at Kitty's bedside, her sister's withered hand in hers. Tears continued to fall from Kitty's open eyes, an endless stream that soaked her pillow in saltwater. Esther tried to dry them at first, but she soon gave up.

Kitty's life would end shortly enough—there was no

question of this—then her soul would be lost to the goblin world forever. Death was painted on her form as surely as night followed day, as winter followed summer. Esther wouldn't allow the Goblin King to take away the bit of youth she had left deep inside her withering form.

There was no time to waste.

Lowering her head to press a kiss to Kitty's hand, Esther whispered, "I will not let you die alone, sister. This much I can promise."

MORNING LIGHT STRUGGLED TO BREAK THROUGH the fog that shrouded the village in its damp embrace as Esther hurried from the house to the market, where she knew those few shops that catered to miners would be open for business. The last of her money would have to be enough for her purposes.

When she met with the sleepy proprietor, he hardly spared Esther a second glance as she recited her list: oil for their largest lamp, several feet of hemp rope, and as many bottles of gin as she could afford. The only candles the shop sold at that hour were made with arsenic, their yellow-green tallow discouraging starving miners from eating their only source of light deep within the earth. Esther bought five and hurried back home.

Assuring herself once more that the house's wards against the goblins were still securely in place, Esther rushed to the cellar and retrieved the wicked fruit. No rot, even after all this time. Peaches, plums, grapes, pears—beneath the lamplight, all shone with tantalizing life, begging Esther to take a bite as she stared down at their glistening skin.

Eat our fruit. The memory of the Goblin King's words traveled through her mind like a ghost. *Everyone does in the end.*

"Not yet," Esther murmured. "Soon, but not yet."

Esther placed the two golden platters on the quilt next to Kitty and got to work. First, moving carefully, she climbed a ladder to attach the oil lamp to the wooden beam overhead, grateful the ceiling in their humble cottage wasn't too high as she reached to secure the lamp with one end of the hemp rope. The cottage was made of stone and brick, not flammable enough for their purposes, and so Esther would have to help the flames.

Winding the remaining length of rope along the beams, Esther balanced one of the candles on the desk at the rope's frayed end, but she didn't light it yet.

Next, Esther gathered every bottle of gin from the house and poured their contents onto the pile of cotton muslin clothing beneath the lamp, the fabric strewn across the floor leading toward the bed, and finally she soaked the mattress itself.

Kitty made no sign that she noticed as Esther poured the liquid over her sister's legs, her torso, even the Bible she held in her withered hands. Fury against an indifferent God filled her when she imagined its gilded cover going up in flame. Esther hesitated, holding the bottle above Kitty's face, and a sob stuck in her throat when she finally poured gin onto her sister's silver hair. The icy, sweet pine scent overpowered the space.

"And now," Esther said, sitting at Kitty's side. Her heart thrummed while remembering the good times, the bad times, but times as sisters, nonetheless. "We feast."

Esther clutched onto an iron crucifix and prayed the

ward would give her enough time to complete the task. With her other hand, she lifted a lush peach, and not once did she tremble as she brought the fruit to her lips. Her pulse steadied, even when she remembered her slaughtered mother and aunt, what the goblins had done to all of them. She sank her teeth into its velvety flesh and colorful light shot through her.

"Delicious," Esther whispered, clenching the crucifix harder.

She focused on her world, attempting with all her might to not cross over just yet as she continued to eat every last piece, so no other innocent would have it. The task wasn't as difficult as she imagined it would be. She hardly wanted to take a breath, much less pause her consumption, and she imagined she could've continued to eat the magical fruit forever. When Esther finished the last grape and the platters lay empty against the gin-soaked quilt, she blinked in dazed amazement.

Esther sighed, turned to Kitty, and gasped. For an instant, her sister appeared young and beautiful once more. Her golden curls fell against rosy, full cheeks, her lips were red as roses, and her aged hands smoothed.

"The goblins' magic has begun its work." Esther stood, knowing she needed to move quickly before she lost her own wits. The iron crucifix was losing its strength to the goblin magic.

Esther lit every candle she had placed around the bed until Kitty lay in a glowing mausoleum of radiance. And lastly, Esther brought the flame to ignite the solitary candle at the end of the frayed hemp rope. As the flames slowly traveled up its length, she soaked her own clothing with the remainder of the last bottle of gin and rested next to her beloved sister, closing her eyes.

"I will join you in your false heaven, sister," she promised, taking Kitty's skeletal hand in hers. "But don't worry, we will not linger there for long. Our souls will be saved."

Esther may have imagined it, but she thought Kitty's hand squeezed hers.

Tears matching Kitty's streamed from her own eyes, but Esther fought against dreams of paradise one last time as she prayed.

"O Lord and Savior," Esther said, "in your arms we are safe. Keep us and we have nothing to fear. Give us up and we have nothing to hope for..."

The flames reached the edge of the ceiling beam—embers of gold and red slowly, *slowly* traveled toward the hanging lamp and its gin-soaked end. Esther's consciousness slipped away, her reality leaving her, her vision filled with summer gardens and flower-dappled forests.

"God have mercy on our souls," she whispered and let go of the crucifix anchoring her to this world.

ESTHER SAT UP. HER ROOM WAS EMPTY. BLINKING in the candlelight, she rose to her feet and took a step forward, then reached for the door. But when she slipped into the stone hallway, Esther found herself beneath a canopy of pink flowers, a grassy path winding before her lit by thousands of fireflies.

Jasmine and honeysuckle surrounded her, along with apple blossoms and summer peaches. "Kitty?" Esther called out and burst into laughter. It was preposterous that her sister would be here. This was only a dream, wasn't it?

The rhythmic sound of ocean waves crashing against

sandy beaches filled the night, and Esther looked up to see an infinity of stars, so close she felt as if she could reach out and touch them. The path continued, vines surrounding her in a comforting embrace of pink blooms, until the sound of laughter mixed with the waves, and she ran, glee coursing through her while she giggled like a child.

"Look, Esther!" Kitty's voice called, her own laughter mixing with her sister's as she raced toward her. "You made the rain stop!"

Esther fell into Kitty's arms. "Did I? Well, I don't know how I did it, so don't ask me to do it again."

"Come with me." Kitty grinned, clasping Esther's hand and tugging her down a glass-flowered trail.

Up ahead, a magical celebration, no equal on earth, was well underway. Esther had reached a true haven. Anything was possible, no unhappiness or grief could ever be entertained here. Happiness blossomed inside her heart. A castle of gold and ivory shone high along a cliff in the distance, while its subjects enjoyed this island miraculously floating above the ocean, its depths glowing with emerald and sapphire orbs. Pillars covered in the same pink blooms encircled the crowd of revelers—each costume more beautiful than the next. Petals fell like confetti along their twirling forms. Golden platters of food and drink were presented at every turn.

Esther looked down at herself to discover she wore a gown of pink and red roses, petals like silk kisses against her skin. Kitty was breathtaking in a dress of peacock feathers. Her torso was wrapped in luminescent greens and blues. Iridescent feathers cascaded to the floor, the eye-like pattern, stunning in the fireflies' glow. As for her hair, amethyst and copper entwined her sunshine locks beneath a crown of gold.

Music as sweet as caramel swept through the night air, its melody impossible to ignore. The drums beat a rhythm that filled Esther's very bones. She laughed again, grasping Kitty by the arm, and pulled her into the crowd of dancers, where nothing but joy reigned.

The sisters danced without tiring as the stars sparkled above them like fireworks. The glowing sea swayed at their feet in time with the music. Nothing seemed real, but it didn't matter. Esther would never be alone again. She had Kitty by her side, her sister young and more vibrant than ever before.

The celebration continued through the night until the rising dawn painted the night sky in golden crimson, a bonfire of delicious warmth, consuming the world in endless summer.

If this was a dream, Esther would gladly slumber for all eternity, falling endlessly...

And then Esther knew no more.

Epilogue

THE GOBLIN KING

Errol was not only Goblin King to his realm. He was its *god*. A word that humans were fond of using. Every time he took a maiden to his realm, they eventually begged and pleaded for God to answer their prayers.

Yet he was the only god here, and Errol would answer their prayers with his own variety of pleasure and pain.

Taking a bite of his emerald apple, he smiled in amusement as he sauntered down the shadowy corridor. Blood and filth stained the walls, the only decoration he relished. Laughter accompanied by screams of agony echoed along the stone, a symphony of pain and delight, depending on what state his precious rodents were in.

"Your Majesty," a servant called, his steps an irritating interruption to his thoughts.

Errol studied the goblin, the pathetically small creature's back hunched at an odd angle. *Julo*o, Errol thought his name was. Simpering, annoying thing.

"What is it?" he snapped, and Juloo tried to stand straight. "I am busy."

The sister who'd vanished from his sight had returned not long ago. He could feel her luxurious essence even now, could smell her bold, defiant scent.

"You will be pleased, Majesty." The creature bowed low. "We have fed a new maiden. She will be here soon."

Errol licked his lips. "Perfect. I hope her hair is as red as blood. I haven't had one with such hair color in quite some time."

"Oh, it is, Your Majesty!" The creature beamed with pride, yet Errol ignored him, and after another two bows, Juloo scurried away.

In the human realm, the women and men considered the Goblin King to be their devil and his servants his demons. Based on the practices those of this realm reveled in, Errol decided they weren't entirely wrong.

He kept his favorite maidens in this particular corridor, the walls lined with cell doors, hundreds of them. He loved every single maiden. He loved toying with them, loved bringing them the utmost pleasure, loved hearing them suffer as he inhaled their essence. They ought to be grateful. After all, they got to be queens for what little time they had left.

It was all too easy, really. Their pathetic need for eternal love was a human emotion effortlessly used for his purposes, and so Errol's world would never cease to exist.

As for the rare few who escaped his palace, Errol always got his revenge. If they preferred being slaughtered over his dungeon, then so be it. The women in his care would continue receiving his pleasure until they withered to dust in their world and their souls officially became his. After them, endless more would find their way to him. So it would continue until the end of time.

While Errol strolled past each of the cells, the maidens reached through the bars. Their torn, white gowns covered in foul stains.

"My king, touch me once again," a maiden with locks of muddy hair pleaded, her nails bloody and her lips cracked.

Another screamed in agony, pressing her face to the bars, and Errol would have almost felt pity for her had he not tired of her already, her lifeforce nearly spent. "Bring me fruit!" she begged. "Please, only one bite. I'll die without it!"

More maidens rocked back and forth inside their tiny prisons, each believing they dwelled in luxury, oblivious to one another as their pleas and shouts continued.

Errol placed a finger over his lips, whispering to each woman that he would return soon.

When he reached the end of the hallway, a single cell made the edges of his mouth curl up farther. This particular room was special—it now held two women whom Errol wished would never fade, if he were honest with himself.

Kitty and Esther.

Esther had, of course, returned, and now, for the first time, he would please her in the way he had her sister. This was his favorite part.

He wondered which one would be sweeter against his tongue, whose life's essence would taste more delicious.

Under his spell, neither sister would care they were married to the same king. Perhaps he would bed them together—tomorrow.

As he stood in front of the gate, his gaze fell to both maidens, and their hair was like golden rays of sun. They sat across from each other while holding hands. Their ripped dresses matched in filth, though Esther's was not yet splattered with blood.

Broad smiles played along their lips, and Errol wormed his fingers through the air, his anticipation rising. The gate unlocked, allowing him to step inside, where both sisters would believe they stood in the middle of somewhere glorious.

"I have yet to reunite with my new queen," Errol purred, kneeling in front of the sisters.

Their heads turned to him, but their eyes didn't shine with devotion as they should have. Something wasn't right. Smoke wafted from their flesh, and Errol blinked, confused by whatever trick was being performed. He was God here. Only he could play tricks in this world.

Bright orange flames crackled to life, licking up the sisters' bodies. Their flesh melted from their bones; their golden hair gone in an instant.

"No!" Errol seethed. "You foolish, wasteful girl!"

Grasping Esther by the shoulders, Errol shook her violently. "You couldn't just eat the fruit, could you?"

There wouldn't be time to drain Esther of her life force now, but Errol tried anyway. She tasted of nectar and pear, her youth and vitality making pleasure soar through him. Yet his feeding ended too quickly, and soon both sisters were nothing more than piles of ash on their prison floor, their souls gone from his world.

The Goblin King curled his lips in disgust. How pathetic humans could be, *murdering* themselves. Wouldn't Esther have wanted to live longer and experience the pleasure he had to offer? This morning he would've taken Esther, and then Kitty at night. Now they were gone—what a dreadful waste. And this cage needed to be filled.

Never mind.

The new guest Juloo spoke of could have it.

"My king!" a maiden called from behind him, her voice full of longing. Errol was reminded that all was not lost. With a shrug, he unlocked the maiden's cell and entered. He would have to rearrange the day's schedule—that was all.

"I am forever at your service," the Goblin King purred with an elaborate bow of his own. "My darling queen."

Afterword

It was said that for one hundred years, nothing grew in the village where the two sisters had perished in a housefire. Eventually everyone moved away, leaving the land a scar of barren earth.

And to this day, if you visit London and look closely at the display in The Tower of London's Jewel House, you can still see two platters of gold that boast craftsmanship far above the rest.

No one is precisely certain where they came from, but who would admit they'd been found amongst the ashes of a humble cottage in a forgotten village?

Preview the next book in
A HORDE OF DEAD POETS
collection!

AVAILABLE NOW

One

The gods slumbered.

Five hundred and thirty years ago had been the last time their gods had awakened, walked among their land, and reduced the nearby villages to cinders. So, the people of Svetl never prayed for mercy, because they already knew their gods were vengeful.

Golden light flickered against the walls of the Great Lodge as hundreds of tallow candles lined the altar. Long, wooden benches remained empty, but they wouldn't for long, not when the villagers of Svetl would spill in, gathering to talk of their recent victories, be it boasting of their fishing, or conquering a neighboring foe.

Svetl was in a time of peace with their neighbors, but as with most things in life, it came in waves.

Eirunn had been born in a time when even her parents hadn't seen battle, yet warriors still trained. But at the age of twelve, she knew she didn't want to hold a shield or sword, battling her brothers and sisters. What Eirunn wanted was to help and to heal. Like Bodin.

She swallowed and walked up the stairs to the platform. Six carvings of their gods and goddesses stood in a *v* formation: Hakan the Father and Supreme one; Gyda the Mother; Sassa the Beauty; Roska the Fierce; Bodin the Caretaker; and Njal the Warrior.

And carved on the platform was a lantern and a shroud of darkness, symbolizing Life and Death. Two entities not of the godly world, but of the living realm. Set apart from the heavens yet still watched.

Eirunn reached out and brushed her fingers along the engraved wood. Bodin's kind and handsome face smiled at his people. She tried to imagine the god, who sought to nurture flora and fauna, so angered that he'd side with destroying them all.

Her skin prickled at the back of her neck, and she spun on her heel, feeling as though someone or something was watching her. "Tyr, if that's you, it isn't funny." He was always trying to scare her, but when he didn't answer and she didn't see his shadow, her heart inched up her throat.

You have nothing to fear, maiden. A deep voice snaked throughout the lodge. Eirunn caught sight of a shadow crawling up the exposed beams, seeming to purposefully remain away from the skylight.

"What are you?" Her voice shook as she backed into the carvings. *No. She hadn't woken one of the gods, had she?* Fearful, she peered around, but nothing else was out of sorts. The candles scarcely flickered, even with the shadow darting around.

The being formed before her, and Eirunn's eyes couldn't focus on the apparition for too long. It was like trying to make a figure out in the early morning light. Her eyes played tricks on her, and it appeared to jerk, or maybe the shadows wavered like a banner in the wind, but when she refocused, the creature was as still as could be.

What am I? The voice rumbled and swiveled around her. *You could ask who I am, but you ask* what? It hummed. *I am the quiet that follows the last beat of a heart. The shadow that waits at the edge of every light. I am the inevitable pause to your fleeting song.*

Eirunn gasped and quickly retreated down the steps toward the long benches. She nearly fell as she bumped into one, but her eyes remained on the undulating figure. "You are...Death." She swallowed roughly and glanced toward the altar.

I am. And I'm here to claim you as my own.

"Am I dead?" Her voice quaked, and she lifted a hand to her throat.

Death laughed coldly. *No, child. I need a maiden, one who can walk between the worlds with me and reap the ripe souls.*

Tears pricked Eirunn's eyes. She was a child of spring, one who cherished life above all else. How could she be a servant of Death? "Why me? Why not someone else?"

The season has passed for my prior reaper, and with no daughter to claim, I have no choice but to search for another. The line of maidens must carry on. The shadows surrounding Death swirled, collecting themselves until a nearly solid figure stood before her. *Be at peace, young one. Death eases the struggle and weight that life brings. It is a noble thing, to die.*

To the villagers, it was an honor to die in battle, while a youth's passing was a bad omen. Eirunn had witnessed Death. Her mother died in childbirth with her little brother, who scarcely lived to see his second month.

"You took my mother away, and my little brother," she said in a rasp.

It was their time, and because I have touched one close to you, it is why I am here. Your soul has been caressed by my presence, marked for me to claim as my own.

"Do I have a choice?" She gritted her teeth, blinking away tears.

No.

Eirunn flopped onto a nearby bench and glanced up at the skylights. In one of the windows, she saw the full moon. She prayed that Bodin would take care of her, and if children were in her future, them too. And she sent up a prayer to Gyda the Mother, for that matter.

"Do you have a name other than Death?"

The apparition hummed in thought, then chuckled. *Some call me Hadeon.*

Fitting, she thought. His moniker meant destroyer.

Although you are my servant, I will allow you a request. Choose how I will appear to you and your family.

Eirunn gawked at the shadows. What did she care, as if he'd be any less of a threat in any form? "A horse as black as night, and a mane that pours down like an ebony waterfall." The moment the words left her mouth the shadows before her turned to smoke, then solidified once more. Before her stood the most impressive horse she'd ever seen.

A stallion with a proud Roman nose and bottomless brown eyes.

He was lovely.

He was *Death*.

"Will anyone else see you?" she whispered and stood. She stepped forward, afraid to touch, but too curious to abstain.

Her hand met a velveteen muzzle, but instead of warmth, there was only coldness.

Only when I want them to. He snorted. *Find me in the barn outside your dwelling and you will begin your lessons.*

The doors to the Great Lodge swung open and the boisterous laughter of her father and the jarl filled the space. Eirunn's eyes widened, panicked that she'd need to explain why she'd brought a horse into the lodge, but when she turned around, there was no one.

Come find me, Hadeon's voice echoed in her mind and when her eyes met her father's his graying brows rose in question.

"What are you doing in here by yourself?" Her father strode forward, flanked by the jarl and another warrior.

Eirunn could lie and say she was just speaking to Bodin, as she had planned to, but for some reason the truth itched the tip of her tongue. "I was talking to Death."

Neither her father nor the men by his side laughed, and she wondered what they knew, if they knew of the maidens before her.

"You spoke to Death?" her father whispered. "Don't jest, dear heart." He closed the space between them and placed his calloused hand on her shoulder. "Why are you really here?"

"I'm not jesting." She glanced up at him. "He said I am his maiden."

The jarl exchanged a glance with the man by his side, then edged forward to her. "Tell no one of what you saw and heard today. Do you understand? Dying is part of our cycle, but if someone knows a maiden is lurking about, they'll come for you in droves. Just as they did Katla."

Eirunn blanched. Katla—the cousin to the jarl—sweet Katla, who was always smiling...She was a maiden?

She had died two months ago, slaughtered in the woods like a common boar. No one knew why, nor who had done it.

With a nod, she turned on her heel to glance back at the gods. All she had wanted to do was pray to them and instead Death had come for her.

ENJOY THESE NOVELLAS IN ANY ORDER!

A HORDE OF
DEAD POETS

BETTER GRAVE THAN THIS
JESSICA CRANBERRY

SOME RAIN MUST FALL
MEG DAILEY

SUCH GOOD BONES
LENN WOOLSTON

IN THE HAUNTS OF GOBLIN MEN
CANDACE ROBINSON
S.G.D. SINGH

DEATH'S MAIDEN
ELLE BEAUMONT

DESCENDANTS OF THE BIG HOUSE
GONZALO FLINT

A HORDE OF DEAD POETS

Acknowledgments

Thank you so much to the readers who wanted a taste of the goblins' fruit!

To our families and friends, you are the light that keeps us going. Carla and Jess, thank you for having us on this journey! And to those whoever come across goblins, steer clear, for you might just become one of the Goblin King's maidens.

About Candace Robinson

Candace Robinson spends her days consumed by words and hoping to one day find her own DeLorean time machine. Her life consists of avoiding migraines, admiring Bonsai trees, watching classic movies, and living with her husband and daughter in Texas—where it can be forty degrees one day and eighty the next!

About S.G.D. Singh

SiriGuruDev Singh lives in New Mexico and Punjab with her husband, two daughters, and various extended relatives and animals.

Stay up to date by visiting www.sgdsingh.com

 instagram.com/sgd_singh

Also by Candace Robinson

Wicked Souls Duology

Vault of Glass

Bride of Glass

Marked by Magic Series

The Bone Valley

Merciless Stars

Her Cruel Dahlias

Cruel Curses Trilogy

Clouded By Envy

Veiled By Desire

Shadowed By Despair

Untamed Darkness Series

And Then There Was Silence

Dearest Clementine: Dark and Romantic Monstrous Tales

These Vicious Thorns: Tales of the Lovely Grim

Savage Delights: Two Dark Tales

Faeries of Oz Series

Lion (Short Story Prequel)

Tin

Crow

Also by S.G.D. Singh

The Infernal Guard Series

Emergence

Descent

Severance

Forsaken

Ravenous

Dracula Retold

The Heart of Babylon

Exiled to Freedom